THE SECRET IN THE CLIFFS

Kristin Tucker

ELECTIO PUBLISHING
first century principles.
a twenty-first century approach.

The Secret in the Cliffs
By Kristin Tucker

ISBN-13: 978-1-63213-528-5

Published by eLectio Publishing, LLC

Little Elm, Texas

http://www.eLectioPublishing.com

5 4 3 2 1 eLP 22 21 20 19 18

Printed in the United States of America.

The eLectio Publishing creative team is comprised of: Kaitlyn Campbell, Emily Certain, Lori Draft, Jim Eccles, Sheldon James, and Christine LePorte.

Publisher's Note

The publisher does not have any control over and does not assume any responsibility for author or third-party websites or their content.

THE SECRET
IN THE CLIFFS

CHAPTER 1

Kyle was surrounded by darkness, but at the moment he was grateful that he was. Outside, he could hear the waves crashing and the wind howling. The problem was that the sound he heard was not the wind or the waves. It sounded more like a repetitive thudding sound that had a fairly steady rhythm. As he held his breath and strained to hear, he noticed another sound that seemed to mingle with the thudding. It reminded him of the sound a bag of concrete made as his dad dragged it across their garage floor. His heart began to beat faster, and he wondered if soon the thumping of his heart would grow as loud as the thudding he heard outside.

Kyle sucked in his breath and did his best to be utterly silent and still. In the quiet, he could sense a pattern in the two sounds. "Thud," pause, "Shuffle." "Thud," pause, "Shuffle." "Thud," pause, "Shuffle." His imagination ran wild trying to figure out what could possibly be making such noises. *It could be a wild animal dragging its prey,* Kyle thought to himself. However, that theory didn't quite fit. It would account for the shuffling he heard, but not for the thudding sound. *Falling rocks could make the thudding sound,*

Kyle reasoned, *but the sound is too rhythmic for it to be falling rocks. And that still doesn't explain the shuffling sound.*

The sounds were getting louder now, and it sent Kyle into panic mode. He knew that just a few feet to his right there was a pile of rocks that formed a makeshift wall. *If I can just get over there without drawing attention to myself,* he pondered, *that would be a great hiding place.* It occurred to him that if he were very careful, he would be able to peek around the end of the wall without being noticed.

He waited patiently and listened to the rhythm of the sounds again. His plan was to dart over behind the rock wall as soon as he heard the next "thud." He figured this was his best option to avoid having his movements heard. At the conclusion of the shuffling sound, Kyle crouched into position. He heard the thud sound, and using his legs like a spring, he launched himself to the edge of the rocks and hurriedly dove behind them. The sound was growing louder by the second, and Kyle could tell that any moment now, whatever was making all the noise would be visible. While he waited, Kyle figured that there were two possibilities he faced. The first was that whatever was out there had been tracking him and it would enter the dark room, only to find him in a matter of minutes. *Sure,* he thought, *I could scurry around the room and try to find other hiding places. But I know it would hear me when I move, so that would not work very well.* The second possible scenario was that whatever it was would just move right past the entrance and keep going. He realized it was entirely possible that he was just being paranoid about being followed.

However, a sinking feeling in the pit of Kyle's stomach told him that there was indeed something out there stalking him. His senses were all on high alert, and he prepared for whatever type of confrontation he might face. He held his breath in order to make as little noise as possible. His ears were tuned to the sounds outside the entrance. The sound of the "thud" and "shuffle" became almost deafening in the silence of the room.

Kyle heard a final "thud," and suddenly a figure appeared in the entrance. The sun, which barely made a dent in the darkness, revealed the silhouette of a man. For a moment, the man stood as still and as quiet as Kyle was behind the rocks. It seemed to be a contest to see who would speak or move first. Kyle was sure he could outlast whoever this stranger was—as long as he didn't stand there *too* long.

From his vantage point, Kyle could see that the man appeared to be tall with an average build. With the light coming in behind him, Kyle saw that the man had what appeared to be a beard. Kyle tried to make out the color of the man's hair in case he ever had the opportunity to identify him. It appeared to be either very light blond or white, but it was difficult for Kyle to be certain. The man was wearing a business suit with a vest underneath his suit jacket. Kyle also noticed that the man wore a pair of glasses that had fallen halfway down his nose. The man appeared to be quite a bit older than Kyle's dad. With this realization, Kyle felt himself relaxing, but only slightly.

The man took a few steps directly ahead of him. He paused and then craned his neck as he glanced around the room. The man spoke, although to Kyle it seemed more like a whisper. "Are you in here?"

Kyle felt a chill run up and down his spine. He contemplated making a break for the entrance, but the thought that kept him from following through seemed almost ridiculous in light of his circumstances. The problem was that Kyle kept picturing himself running past the man and accidentally knocking him over in the process. Kyle realized that if this really was an older man, even if the man *was* stalking him for some strange reason, he would feel horrible if he was responsible for the man getting hurt. He decided to remain silent for a few minutes longer and waited for the man to make the next move.

Kyle watched as the man turned to his right and walked a few steps in that direction. The man appeared to be straining to see anything. Kyle was certain that coming into the dark space after being out in the bright sun was causing the man's vision to be impaired. Kyle had experienced that same problem when he first entered the darkness. It had taken several minutes before his eyes had truly adjusted and he was able to see without the aid of a flashlight. When Kyle thought of the flashlight, he realized that he was still holding it in his hand. He came to the conclusion that if it were absolutely necessary, he could use the flashlight as a means of protecting himself. *Of course,* he reassured himself, *that would be the absolute last resort.*

The man turned to his left and was now facing the direction of the rock wall that Kyle was hiding behind. Once again, Kyle sucked in his breath and tried to be as still as humanly possible. Kyle noticed that the man was not actually moving toward him, but was staying in one spot, obviously trying to listen for any sounds that would indicate someone else was there. "Young man," the older man said, speaking just above a whisper this time, "if you are in here, please come out. I will not hurt you." There was a pause, as if the man was still hoping for a response. When Kyle remained quiet, the man spoke again, saying, "I only wish to speak with you."

For some reason, Kyle *almost* felt like he could trust the man. He considered the possibility of stepping out from behind the rock wall and showing himself to the man. *What's the worst he could do to me?* Kyle reasoned. *He's an old man.* However, Kyle wasn't feeling quite brave enough to make that step, so he remained in his hiding spot and said nothing. He watched as the man turned back in the direction of the entrance. It appeared to Kyle that he was giving up and was planning to leave. Kyle felt some of the tension leave his body. He felt his muscles relax some, which was a good thing, because the way he had been crouched down was causing his muscles to ache severely. He was anxious to be able to stand up and move, but he had decided that there was *no way* he was moving until that man left.

"Well, I can see that you are not ready to speak to me yet," he heard the man say with a sigh. "However, there will come a time when you *will* speak with me." With that, the man retreated back to the entrance. He paused there briefly, turning around to scan the darkness once more. Kyle imagined that the man was hoping Kyle might change his mind. When he was met with only silence, the man suddenly pirouetted and walked out into the bright sunshine. Kyle felt an immense relief wash over him, and he collapsed onto the dusty ground. He listened for the now familiar "thud," pause, "shuffle" to determine whether the man was actually moving away from his hiding place. Kyle decided it would be best to wait for the sounds to dissipate before he even attempted heading outside.

The sounds of the man walking away grew more faint and, within moments, Kyle heard nothing but the wind and the waves outside. He flicked his flashlight on and made a sweeping motion around the room. He could see that there was nothing and no one lurking in the shadows, so he made the decision to make his exit.

As he crept over to the entrance, he came to the realization that he would have to scan the area outside from a hidden vantage point before he felt it was safe to leave. At the entrance, he hid his body to the right of the jagged entrance and peeked around the corner. He saw nothing, but still he had to be sure. He listened carefully for any sounds that might hint that someone was still lurking out there. He heard nothing, but he decided that it would be best to be absolutely certain. He got down on all fours and crawled across to the other side of the opening. Kyle shuddered and paused as the thought occurred to him that he was not being very stealthy. In fact, he had been making an awful lot of racket as his feet dragged behind him on the sandy rock. He decided that, in order to make the least possible sound, it would be best to lift his knees slightly off the ground when he moved forward.

Kyle repeated this action until he made it safely across to the other side. Once there, he sat in silence and waited to see if he had drawn the attention of anyone lurking outside. When no one appeared, he oh-so-carefully peered around the wall on this side of the entrance. He saw nothing in that direction that caused him any concern. At this point, Kyle believed that he was in the clear. He stood upright and stretched out his aching legs. When he felt like they were back to normal, he made his move and stepped forward into the blinding sun.

Kyle could see spots before his eyes as they adjusted to brightness. He told himself that the wise thing to do would be to not try to navigate the steep path to his left until his eyes were fully accustomed to the light. Although he felt a sense of urgency to leave, the thought of stepping on a loose rock and tumbling to the rocky beach below was not a welcome one. He determined that he would take a few minutes to enjoy the view around him. The sound of the waves crashing on the beach below had a calming effect on him, and he felt an increasing sense of peace overtaking his mind.

In the distance, Kyle could see what appeared to be three young men riding the waves on their surfboards. He watched as they held their arms out, parallel to the water, which enabled them to keep their balance. Kyle pondered the sport of surfing. He was amazed at how these guys were able to jump up on their boards when a wave first began to swell. He had attempted it himself a few times, but he had never quite gotten the hang of it. He remembered being frustrated at his limitations. Many of his friends were surfers, and because he was unable to even get into a standing position on a surfboard, this precluded him from ever joining them. Kyle sighed, but then reminded himself that if he was always hanging out with his buddies, he would never have had the opportunity to make the discovery that he had.

Kyle watched the surfers ride the wave the rest of the way in. He saw one of the guys crouch down and the surfboard sped to the shore. The other two did the same, and soon Kyle saw that they had landed safely on the shore as well. Kyle's attention was drawn elsewhere, and he watched as a young couple strolled along the shore with bare feet. Occasionally, the man would reach down and scoop up some water and toss it in the direction of his girlfriend. Kyle could hear the woman screech when the cold water hit her. Kyle couldn't help but laugh out loud.

His laugh startled him back to his current reality. Kyle remembered the man appearing in the darkness and how terrified he had felt about possibly being discovered. "I need to get moving!" Kyle told himself. He turned to the left and made sure he was able to see the path and the steep slope down to the beach clearly before he proceeded. Kyle could tell that his eyes had indeed gotten readjusted to the sunlight, so now he felt safe in making his way back down the path.

There were two directions Kyle could take on the path to get back to the bike rack. One was a little wider and much easier to navigate. The drawback was that it took more time to follow the path that way. Kyle knew that if he followed the path around the side of the cliff and then continued down the slope on the backside of the cliff, he would get to the bike rack much faster. The trouble with going that direction was that the path was very jagged in places and it was hard to navigate, and thus more dangerous.

Kyle decided that because he had been followed by the older man, it would be best for him to take the shorter route and leave as quickly as possible. He took several steps and approached a section of the path that was severely narrowed compared to the rest of it. Kyle knew he needed to be extra careful while navigating this particular stretch of the path. On previous visits, he had learned that it was best to turn sideways and hug the wall of the cliff next to him. Kyle knew this would slow him down, but he rationalized that it was better to take the extra time than it would be to go tumbling down the steep walls of the cliff. He shuffle-stepped on his tiptoes, moving ever so carefully. It seemed to him that his hands would never get used to the sharp feel of the rocks as he clung to them for safety.

Once Kyle had made it safely past the narrowed section of the path, he gave himself permission to pick up his speed. Suddenly, Kyle heard a loud "Whump!" behind him, and he turned quickly to see what might have made the noise. A man crouched there on the path, not more than ten feet away from Kyle. He appeared to be in his mid-thirties and had extremely dark brown hair. Kyle could tell instantly that this was not someone he was familiar with. Kyle noticed that the man stared at him with the same look a tiger has right before it pounces on its prey. Kyle was absolutely stunned at the notion that this man was out to get him for some reason.

Kyle searched his surroundings, trying to get a grasp on where the man had come from. *It doesn't make sense at all!* Kyle thought. *I looked every which way, and there was no sign of anyone around.* Kyle gazed directly above where the man was and noticed a small ledge that the man had most likely been standing on before he had hurled himself to the ground.

Kyle quickly sized up the distance between the dark-haired man and himself. There were two reasons he knew he held an advantage over this guy. The first was that because he had traveled this path so many times, it was highly likely that he would be able to navigate the way back down the cliff far easier than his pursuer. The second, and, at this point, probably the most vital, was that he had already crossed the portion of the path that was so narrow. Kyle figured that the guy, being a good twenty years older than him, would have a far more challenging time holding onto the rocks with his hands. *Even if it's not as hard for him as I think it might be,* Kyle thought, *it will still take him longer to cross that narrow ledge. That will give me a good head start.*

Kyle raced ahead, willing himself not to look back. He knew that if he did look back it would only cause him to feel more panicked than he already did. The path began to slope downward at a much steeper angle than before, and Kyle did his best to keep his speed up without losing control of where his feet were landing. There were many rocks strewn about that at a normal speed would not have been difficult to avoid. At this speed, however, every step he took seemed to be a near miss of the rocks.

Kyle heard a noise behind him, and he realized that it was the man who had been chasing him. In Kyle's mad rush to escape he had been singularly focused on getting back down to his bike. Somehow, in spite of that focus, it registered in Kyle's brain that the man had shouted, "Whoa!" Kyle had the feeling that something bad was either about to happen or had already happened to the guy. Kyle felt a strange concern for the man grow over him. He stopped for a brief moment to see if the guy was still standing on the path or if he had fallen down the jagged cliffside. Kyle caught sight of the man holding onto the rocks with his hands, just as Kyle had done. It appeared that the man's right foot had slipped a bit, but he had not fallen. Kyle sighed and began moving down the path again. *There is no way I am going to let him catch me!* Kyle thought.

Kyle came to another turn in the path which would lead him around to the back of the cliff. He knew that the path on the back side of the cliff was far smoother, even though it was pretty steep. It seemed to Kyle that the drastic slope of the path would actually work in his favor at this moment. He realized that with no rocks obstructing his way, he would be able to run at full speed. He also knew that the effect of the pull of gravity would increase his momentum. Kyle felt tempted to look back to see where the man was, but he fought the temptation and kept running. It wasn't long before Kyle had reached the bottom of the path. He saw his bike parked in the rack and he headed for it with his legs pumping as hard and fast as they could.

Once Kyle reached the bike rack, he quickly dialed the combination on the lock and gave the chain an impatient tug. The lock got stuck in the spokes of the wheels, and once again, Kyle yanked on the chain until it ripped right through the spokes. The lock came flying back toward him, dangerously close to his head. Kyle breathed a sigh of relief that the lock had missed him and quickly hopped on his bike. He turned in time to see the dark-haired man reach the bottom of the path. Kyle knew there was no way the guy could catch him now. He gave a quick wave to the man, as if he were taunting him. With that, Kyle rode through the parking lot, past many happy beachgoers who obviously had no idea what he had just encountered. Kyle's last thought as he turned out onto the highway was that he envied them their tranquility

****

Kyle rode as fast as he could in the direction of his home. As much as he loved his secret place, right now, the only thing he wanted was to be as far away from there as possible. He felt as if he had dodged a bullet.

As he rode, Kyle barely noticed the cars that whizzed past him on the highway. He was lost in thought about all that had occurred over the last couple of hours. When he tried to recall how it had all played out, he remembered that he had only been inside for a matter of minutes before he started hearing the strange sounds outside. He had an image in his mind of trying to get his eyes adjusted to the dark before moving forward. He knew the layout of the room well, but not quite well enough to find his way around there without being able to see. His plan had been to scan all the areas of the room until he knew that he was seeing everything clearly enough to proceed to the next room. Once he entered the next room, Kyle had intended to switch on his flashlight and explore to his heart's content. Of course, he knew in the back of his mind that he only had a limited time before he had to get home. However, he had every intent of making the time that he did have count.

Kyle had been particularly excited about his explorations that day because he had recently come across some fascinating (and perplexing) discoveries. When he had first entered the dark space, he had full confidence that he would find something just as unique on this trip. He remembered thinking that he would have to keep an eye on the time. His mother was adamant about him being home for dinner on time. Kyle realized that, during his explorations, it would be very easy to forget to look at his watch. That was something that he always fretted about when he came to the cliffs to explore. A few moments ago, Kyle had peeked at his watch to see what time it was and realized that he would probably be in the doghouse when he got home. "I certainly didn't plan for things to happen this way," Kyle told himself.

His thoughts circled back around to the older man entering the cave. Kyle recalled that the man had said he wanted to talk with him. He had also said that it was obvious that Kyle was not ready to talk, but that "there will come a time when you *will* speak with me." The words sent shivers all through Kyle's body. He shuddered and suddenly became aware that he had let go of the handlebars. The bike began to wobble slightly, and Kyle fought to regain control. Once he had steadied himself, he returned to his thoughts. Kyle couldn't imagine what that man could possibly want to talk with him about. He had never seen the man before and he certainly had never spoken with him before. Kyle was sure he would have recognized that accent. Kyle figured that if he knew nothing about the man, then it was highly unlikely that the man knew anything about him. "So why was he following me?" Kyle asked himself.

There was something else that was troubling him. The second man had appeared seemingly out of nowhere, and there was a lapse in time between the older man leaving and the dark-haired man appearing. This made Kyle wonder to himself, *Are the two of them working together, or was it just a coincidence that they were both following me on the same day?*

Kyle used logic to try to solve the perplexing issue. On one hand, the two men seemed to have entirely different personalities, as well as different methods of approaching him. To Kyle, this indicated that the two were working separately. The older man had seemed determined to speak with him, but not to the point that he was willing to force the issue. It was obvious, however, that the younger man had been bent on getting his hands on Kyle no matter what he had to do. The second possibility was that the two men *were* working together. *That would explain why they both came after me at the same place and pretty close to the same time,* Kyle reasoned. If that were true, though, it would have made more sense if they had come after him *together.* Kyle couldn't make the pieces of the puzzle fit no matter which way he looked at it, and it frustrated him.

He shook his head. He realized that at this point he did not have near enough information to be able to figure out what was going on. Kyle, being the curious sort, was not going to be able to let this go very easily. However, he was certain that all he was doing at this point was spinning his wheels. He tried to focus on the task at hand, which was getting home. He heard the rhythmic "whoosh, whoosh, whoosh" of the bicycle tires moving along the pavement. Somehow, the sound lulled him into a bit of a trance.

Kyle had been riding on the shoulder to the right of the highway lanes. He really had not been paying too much attention to the traffic that had been going by. His thoughts had preoccupied every bit of his focus and energy. Suddenly, out of the corner of his eye, Kyle noticed that a large white car was driving right alongside of him. Although he wasn't paying very close attention, he was aware that, based on the body style, it was an Oldsmobile. Kyle's dad was a fan of vintage cars, and he had been keen on passing that information along to Kyle. Kyle pondered what it was about this particular car that was drawing his attention. It dawned on him that the car was driving very slowly, almost as if to match the speed that

Kyle was going with his bike. This caused Kyle to look through the window of the car across to the driver's side of the vehicle.

What he saw startled him so much that he reacted with his instincts instead of his logic. Kyle had noticed two things: The first was that he was nearly at the turn-off for his subdivision. The second was that there was a man driving the car. A quick glimpse of the driver revealed that it was the older man he had seen up at the cliffs. The sight of the man caused Kyle to swerve and lose control of his bike. The next thing he knew, he and the bike were heading toward a rail fence that lined one of the properties on the outskirts of his subdivision. Kyle felt all of the bumps in the grassy ditch as he flew over them. Unfortunately, the bumps caused Kyle to lose what little control he had left of the bike. Kyle saw that he was fast approaching the fence, and he realized that he was not going to be able to stop the bike in time. Before he could even let out a shout, he and the bike collided with the fence and Kyle was knocked out cold.

CHAPTER 2

K yle couldn't tell which was louder, the slap-slap-slap of his feet on the pavement or the thumping of his heart. He was trying to run as fast as he had when he was trying to escape the dark-haired man on the path at the cliff.

Kyle remembered waking up and realizing that he had been temporarily knocked out by the collision with the fence. When he came to, the white Oldsmobile was nowhere to be seen. It had taken Kyle several minutes to feel like everything was coming back into focus. Once he had been able to stand without feeling like everything was spinning around him, he had surveyed the damage that had been done to his bike. It seemed to Kyle that the impact had caused some slight damage to the handlebars and part of the frame below the handlebars. He examined those areas a little more thoroughly and concluded that the bike was still in working condition. Kyle realized that he was feeling pretty sore from the impact and the subsequent tumble to the ground, so he decided that it would be best to leave his bike there for the time being and go back later to get it. Even though it had looked as if the older man had left, Kyle could not be certain that he was not parked somewhere, waiting to see which direction Kyle would take.

Kyle now looked at the watch on his left wrist and realized that he was *very* late for dinner. "Move a little faster, feet!" he exclaimed. As he looked at the traitors that refused to cooperate, he noticed how filthy his sneakers were. That reminded him that the rest of him was just as grubby as his shoes. "Ugh!" He rounded the corner from 4th Street and took a left onto Sycamore Drive. Another two blocks, then a right onto Shady Lane and he would be just about home free. Almost. He realized that from now on he would have to be constantly on the lookout for the older man in the white Oldsmobile and the dark-haired man.

He was approaching the entrance of his driveway when he heard a familiar voice calling out his name. Kyle was startled out of his train of thought by the voice of the girl next door. Kaitlin was cutting across her yard and picked up her pace in order to catch Kyle before he got into his house.

"Where have you been?" she asked. She grabbed him by the shoulders, looked him straight in the eyes, and said, "Your mother has been looking for you and she is fit to be tied!"

"I know, I know!" he huffed. "I'm going to have a lot of explaining to do."

"Well, let me go in with you, and hopefully she won't be so hard on you," said Kaitlin.

"OK, Kaitlin, you can come in with me, but don't get mad at me if you have to see the wrath of Mom."

Kaitlin smiled, and her eyes lit up as she realized that he had agreed. She grabbed his hand and reached for the door handle, but then stopped short. Standing right in front of him and blocking his way, she whispered, "Where were you anyway? You are terribly dirty."

Kyle looked down first at his mud-splattered white T-shirt, then to his jeans and sneakers that were fully covered with drying mud. "Um, Kaitlin, I can't really tell you that," he said, avoiding her gaze. He knew she wasn't going to like that answer.

She looked at him with pleading, puppy-dog eyes and said very sweetly, "Pleeeease, Kyle, please tell me."

Kyle still refused to look at her and answered, "No, Kaitlin, I can't. It's a secret."

Kaitlin's eyes flashed with frustration and anger and she huffed, "Fine! Then you can face your mother all by yourself!"

"Oh, Kaitlin, you're making this impossible! Don't you think that if I could tell you I would?" he pleaded.

"No, I don't!" she exclaimed. "I think you want to keep this so-called secret all to yourself. I've always shared my secrets with you, Kyle."

He had to admit she was right about that. They had known each other since they were in kindergarten. Now they were in sixth grade, and he could not ever remember a time that she had kept a secret from him. *Doggone it!* he thought. *I have to tell her.* He was silent for a beat and then he said, "All right, Kaitlin. I will share my secret with you. But I can't tell you now. It's something I have to *show* you."

At first, she didn't seem satisfied with his answer, but then a look of resignation came over her face. "Fine, but you better not break your promise!"

****

It was Saturday and Kyle had long since finished all of his homework for the weekend. He had read some of his favorite books about archaeology and the hidden treasures that, over the years, men had unearthed. Those stories were the most fascinating to him. The pictures he saw in these books seemed almost beyond belief. How was it, he wondered, that these ancient artifacts had gone undiscovered all these years?

Kyle reclined on his pillow and began to read where he had left off. He was so engrossed in his book that he could only faintly distinguish that his mom was calling out his name from the bottom of the stairs. "Kyle. Kyle. Kyyyle."

He jumped off his bed and threw open his bedroom door. "I'm here," he shouted down to his mom.

"Well," his mom said, "I thought you had snuck out through your bedroom window and gone on one of your little adventures."

"Ha-ha! Very funny Mom," he replied. "I'm a little sore to be going on any expeditions today."

His mom laughed and said, "I suppose you're right about that. All right then, as long as you're here, why don't you go ahead and wash up for dinner. When you come downstairs you can set the table."

By the time they sat down to eat dinner, it was nearly 5:30. His mom had fixed Kyle's favorite dinner tonight, and boy, oh boy, was he happy! The homemade pizza had just the right amount of pepperoni and lots of mozzarella cheese. Kyle's stomach growled, and he thought to himself that he couldn't wait to dive into that pizza.

His mom grinned from ear to ear when she saw how excited Kyle was for dinner. It was typical to hear moans and groans from him when it came to the dinner menu. She had decided that, because it was Saturday and she had a little extra time, she would take the time and make something she knew Kyle would really love. As Kyle's mom watched her son excitedly grab his plate to fill it with pizza, she was glad she had put in the extra effort.

They sat down and thanked God for the meal before them, and at the end, Kyle said a boisterous "Amen!" As soon as the prayer was done, he scooped up three pieces of the pizza and began to devour them.

His mom laughed and said, "Slow down, Kyle, before you choke yourself." Kyle smiled sheepishly at her but then continued to attack his pizza. "Oh brother," his mom said.

While they ate, she asked Kyle what he had been doing to occupy himself in his room. He told her that he had been reading his books about archaeology and how much he loved looking at the pictures of the artifacts.

His mom shook her head in an acknowledging way and said, "You know, when you come home all full of mud, I often wonder if you've been out trying to dig up some buried treasure."

Kyle was somewhat startled by her comment and for a moment he held his breath. *If only she knew,* Kyle thought. He answered her by saying, "Yeah, it's something like that. I never find anything great like they find in the books though."

His mom seemed to accept that answer, and then she was on to something else. "I almost forgot to tell you. I know we usually go to church on Sunday mornings, but since your father is stuck working every weekend, I decided we should try to go to the Saturday night service. At least this way he will get out of work in time to meet us there. It doesn't give us much time to get this cleaned up." She glanced at her watch and said, "Well, never mind. We will just put the leftover pizza in the refrigerator and we can wash the dishes later. We really should leave in about twenty minutes. The service starts at seven thirty. I realize this is very late notice, but why don't you run next door and ask Kaitlin if she would like to go with us."

"Thanks, Mom," Kyle responded. "I bet she will be happy to come to the service with us."

Kyle stepped out onto the front porch with an enormous grin on his face. He ran so fast through Kaitlin's front yard that he nearly tripped over the family's dog. Kyle thought their dachshund was a cute little guy, but that incessant barking drove him crazy. Chester barked at ev-er-y-thing. The fact that he was so small and that he had mostly black fur made him nearly impossible to see when it was dark. The dog yipped at Kyle, more than likely out of fear than because of any actual injuries.

"Aww, Chester, I'm sorry. I really didn't see you there," he said as he leaned over to pet the little creature. Chester rolled over onto his back with his legs sticking straight up in the air. Kyle knew this meant that he was supposed to rub the dog's belly. So Kyle did exactly that. Within a matter of seconds, the two were friends again. Kyle gave Chester a little pat on the head and said, "I better go, buddy. I have to get Kaitlin and get back home." Chester sniffed at him, almost as if he was put off, and then waddled away.

Kyle approached his neighbor's front door and rang the bell. He heard a female voice call out from a distance, "Just a minute." He heard feet scurrying toward the door, and then it opened with a whoosh. "Oh, hello, Kyle," Kaitlin's mom said. "What can I do for you?"

"Hello, Mrs. Davenport. I came over to ask if Kaitlin might be able to go church with us," he answered.

She hesitated only for a moment and then said, "Umm, sure, Kyle. It's short notice, but that should be fine. We didn't have anything planned anyway." She turned away from the door toward the back of the house and hollered, "Kaitlin . . ." When there was no answer, Mrs. Davenport looked back at Kyle and said, "Give me one minute. I'll go get her for you."

As she strode down the hallway that led to Kaitlin's bedroom, Kyle had a funny thought. Kaitlin's mom's last name was Davenport. He knew her first name was Sophie because he had heard Kaitlin's dad call her that. Sophie . . . Davenport. Kyle had to stifle a chuckle. It *was* a funny name, after all. All he could figure was that when her parents named her Sophie, they didn't plan on her marrying a man with the last name of Davenport.

Kyle's thoughts were interrupted when Kaitlin came charging toward the front door. "Hey, Kyle," she said, "Mom told me we're going to church. Sounds like fun."

"Good," he replied, "but we better get going or we'll be late and then Mom will have my hide."

The two of them ran back to Kyle's house just as his mom was backing the car out of the garage. She smiled at Kaitlin and said, "I'm so glad you could come tonight, Kaitlin. All right, you two, hop in. If we don't leave now we will be late. We don't want your dad to be waiting for us too long."

The ride to the church was fairly short, so they didn't have much time to talk. Kaitlin was just whispering to Kyle, "Now we can go on our adventure!" when they pulled into the church parking lot. Kyle held his finger up to his mouth to silence her. He mouthed the word "later" and she nodded as if to say "OK."

The three of them got out of the car and walked to the entrance of the church. Kyle could hear music playing in the background. Kaitlin held her hands up to cover her ears. "Wow!" she exclaimed. "Those drums sure are loud."

"If you think they're loud now," Kyle retorted, "just wait until we get into the sanctuary." Kaitlin rolled her eyes but let her hands down.

As they entered the front door, Kyle saw his dad standing just to the left of the sanctuary. "Hey, Dad," Kyle said as he leaned in to give his father a hug.

"Hello, Kyle," he said as he ruffled his son's hair. He turned to Kaitlin. "Kaitlin, I'm so glad that you were able to come tonight."

"Me too, Mr. Marshall," said Kaitlin with a smile.

Kyle's mom leaned over and hugged her husband and said, "I'm glad to see you too, Mr. Marshall." He tweaked her nose and gave her a kiss, and then led the three of them to a row in the back of the room.

Kyle had to admit that he was relieved. He had never really cared for sitting in the very front of the room. There was just something awkward, he had decided, about having the pastor staring down at you through the whole sermon. They all took their seats, with Kyle sitting at the very end of the pew. The music was still playing and the man on the stage encouraged them all to stand and sing with them.

In the middle of singing "Amazing Grace," Kyle saw a tall figure walk briskly past him. Kyle was focusing on the words he was singing, but there was something about that figure that caught his eye. He tried to follow the man's path down the aisle and watched as he took his place next to a much shorter man. He watched as the two exchanged a few words. He felt perplexed by his sudden urge to watch the man. There was something about him, something familiar. Kyle's mind raced as he tried to figure out where he might have seen him before. It was very difficult to concentrate on singing the words of the song while searching his mind for any reasons that the man seemed familiar to him. He finally gave up and turned his attention back to the screen with the words on it.

Then a memory surfaced, and he slapped his hand over his mouth to cover a startled cry.

Kaitlin, who was sitting next to him, caught his reaction. "Kyle, what on earth is going on?" she whispered in his ear.

Kyle could only stare in disbelief at the man. *What is* he *doing here?* he thought.

Kaitlin tugged at his shirt sleeve. "Kyle?"

All Kyle could do now was to point in the man's general direction. With wide eyes, he looked at Kaitlin and said, "It's *HIM!*"

CHAPTER 3

Kaitlin stood dumbfounded for what seemed like an eternity. She turned and gave Kyle a puzzled look, but he was not looking back at her. He was staring at that man. If Kaitlin didn't know better, she would have thought he seemed *scared*. She tapped him on the shoulder to get his attention, but he never batted an eye. "Kyle," she whispered. Still no response. She tugged on the sleeve of his shirt, but he couldn't unlock his eyes from the man. *Very strange,* she thought. *He doesn't seem terrifying to me.*

She was not one to give up easily, so she placed her hand on the top of his head and turned it until he was facing her. It took a few moments before Kyle's eyes followed the direction of his head. Once she felt like she had at least most of his attention, she leaned in close to his face and whispered vehemently, *"WHO IS HE?"*

Kyle noticed his dad was looking at him, and the look said that he was not very happy. Kyle's eyes darted back to Kaitlin and he hissed, "Not now!"

"But Kyle . . ." she said. "You looked terrified when you saw that man. I'm worried!"

Kyle noticed his dad was still glaring at him. He knew that look, and he knew that when his dad looked like that he meant business. He leaned over to Kaitlin and hurriedly said, "I'll tell you tomorrow, I promise. Come over and meet me in my backyard and I'll tell you the whole story."

Once more he looked in the man's direction and then he continued, "You're not going to believe it anyway."

"This stinks!" Kaitlin whined. "First I have to wait for you to show me your little secret. Now this happens, and you can't tell me about this either."

"I wish I could explain it all to you right now, Kaitlin," Kyle said, trying to soothe her. "I promise I will tell you, but not tonight."

"Fine," Kaitlin said with an air of frustration. She remained silent during the remainder of the service. Kyle could tell she was angry with him for making her wait, but what could he do? This was not exactly the time or place for the discussion they would need to have.

When the service was over, Kyle watched as the tall man and his short companion walked down the aisle past them and to the sanctuary's exit. Neither of the men looked in his direction as they passed the row where Kyle sat. He breathed a sigh of relief and felt his body relax. It appeared that the man had not recognized Kyle after all. *Whew!* thought Kyle. *That was close.*

The four of them exited the sanctuary, then made their way out the front door of the church and headed toward the two cars in silence. Once they reached Mr. Marshall's car, his wife kissed him on the cheek and said, "See you at home."

"All right, dear," he replied.

On the ride home Kyle caught Kaitlin peeking at him and looking as if she were about to burst. He patted her on the shoulder as they pulled into their driveway. "Tomorrow," he whispered, "I promise." Kaitlin pouted but agreed.

Mr. Marshall had pulled in ahead of the three of them and parked up close to the garage. He opened the garage door so his wife could pull inside, but Mrs. Marshall stopped the car in the driveway so Kaitlin could hop out. As Kaitlin started heading toward her front door, she said, "Good night, Kyle. See you tomorrow. Good night, Mr. and Mrs. Marshall. Thank you for bringing me to the service tonight."

As Mr. Marshall exited the car, he smiled at Kaitlin. "We were glad to have you come with. Please tell your mom and dad hello for me."

"I will," Kaitlin responded.

Kyle watched as Kaitlin bounded through her front yard. As she got near to the front porch, he noticed that she stopped suddenly. He saw her lean down with a smile on her face as she spoke softly to her pet. Chester, who was always eager to get his belly rubbed, plopped down on the grass right in front of her. Kyle could hear Kaitlin giggle as his tiny little legs stuck straight up in the air and his tongue hung limply out of the side of his mouth. As Kyle watched her rub the little dog's belly, he would have sworn he saw that animal smiling. Kaitlin stood up and said, "Come on, Chester. It's time to go inside." She gave a quick farewell wave to Kyle and he waved back.

Kyle and his dad walked toward the garage to go inside. His mom had already parked her car and was walking into the house. Kyle and his dad followed her up the step and into the kitchen.

Once the door was closed and secured for the night, Kyle walked through the kitchen, then into the living room. The room was dark except for a small nightlight that allowed him to see his way to the bottom of the stairs.

The night had seemed long and exhausting, so he immediately headed up the stairs for his room. "I'm going to bed," he said to his mom and dad. "Love you."

His mom looked a bit surprised, but shrugged her shoulders and said, "OK, honey. Sleep well."

"Good night, son," his dad said.

As soon as he was in his room he collapsed onto his bed. He was certain that the stress of the evening would cause him to fall asleep the second his head hit the pillow. That was not in the cards tonight, he soon found out. Over and over his mind replayed the scenario at church when he had first noticed the tall man. He tossed and turned while his mind attempted to process what it meant that the man was at his church. *It would be one thing,* he thought, *if I had seen the man come to a service before. I've never seen him anywhere in town before. If he was a local, I should have seen him somewhere in town before he appeared in the cave the other day.*

For the life of him, Kyle could not figure out what business would have brought the man to his town. For that matter, Kyle was perplexed as to how the man even knew about his secret place. As far as Kyle knew, not one single person in his town knew about it. He had never so much as seen a stray dog walking by, and he had been there quite often over the last few months. How the older man and the other younger man had come to find the place was quite a mystery.

Kyle's first impression of the tall man was that he had a grandfatherly look to him. From Kyle's point of view, he actually looked like a taller, slimmer version of Santa Claus. He was not someone who instilled a sense of fear.

The other man, though, was a completely different story. The younger man had hair as black as night and dark brown eyes. Kyle remembered those eyes very well. They seemed cold and hard, as if two pieces of coal had been shoved into the man's eye sockets. Kyle had felt certain that the man's glaring eyes could have bored right into him. It was obvious to Kyle that the younger man did not approve of Kyle being there.

That man has some nerve, Kyle thought. *I found that place long before they did! If anyone doesn't belong there, it's them!* It was easy for him to feel bold now that the two men were not around. He had to admit, though, that he was hoping he would not run into either of them again. All he wanted was to be left alone to do his exploring.

Kyle thought about Kaitlin coming with him to his secret spot. At first, he was a little worried that he may be endangering her by allowing her to come with him. But as he considered the scenario a little more, he thought it would probably be better for her to be there. After all, he couldn't imagine that those two men would try any funny business with a girl around.

With that settled in his mind, he told himself he needed to get some sleep. It was getting close to one a.m. He had promised Kaitlin he would meet her in the backyard. If she came over tomorrow (or today) and found out that he was still sleeping, she would hit the roof. He rolled over on his back and put the pillow over his head to keep the moonlight out of his face. He started to count sheep but didn't make it past five before he was sound asleep.

CHAPTER 4

Kyle awoke late the next morning. When he realized how very late it was, he jumped out of bed and scurried over to his dresser. He quickly chose a midnight-blue T-shirt that said, "Archaeologists Have the Best Digs." He threw on the T-shirt along with his jeans and socks and ran downstairs. He hadn't told Kaitlin a specific time to meet him, but he knew her well enough to know that as soon as she saw him outside she was certain to come over.

"Good morning, Mom," Kyle hollered from the kitchen. He could hear the TV playing in the living room and he knew his mom had tuned in to watch one of the televised broadcasts of a sermon from the local church. His dad had left for work a couple of hours ago. As Kyle thought of his dad, he felt a slight sense of sadness wash over him. He missed having his dad around on the weekend.

Kyle remembered that when he was younger, he and his dad would go on little adventures in which they would find places they could search for treasure of any kind. They would bring a metal detector and many times had unearthed strange relics. Very rarely did they find anything of value. However, one time they found an old coin that Mr. Marshall was certain would bring a high-dollar value. He had insisted that Kyle clean the coin until it was restored as closely as possible to its original beautiful silver shine. He had also insisted that Kyle keep the coin. He wanted Kyle to save it until he was older and hopefully pass it along to his children.

On Saturdays he and his dad used to wake up early in the morning so they could pack all their gear and a picnic lunch in the car. They would grab a quick bite to eat for breakfast, but Kyle was never very hungry. All he could think about was getting to their favorite spot and what kind of fun they would have that day. The beach they went to was just a few miles from their house, but back then it seemed like it took forever to get there. When they finally pulled up in the parking lot next to the beach, Kyle would immediately jump out of the back seat and run out onto the sand. He was intent on finding the perfect spot for their dig. His dad would have to call him back to the car so he could help carry their equipment. Kyle would grumble about having to haul everything to the beach, but his dad would remind him that they wouldn't be able to find their treasures without the equipment. "Responsibilities come first, son," his dad would say. "When you do your work with all your heart, it allows you to enjoy the fun even more."

They had all kinds of territory to explore at the beach. Kyle remembered that from one week to the next they could search the beach and find something different every time. Sometimes they would find nothing at all, and then the very next time they would find all kinds of items. The only thing Kyle and his dad could figure was that the waves crashing up on the beach carried things that people had lost while they were out cruising in their boats. The other possibility was that people accidentally left things behind when they packed up to go home. It seemed that watches were one of the most common items left behind. The metal detector picked up so many watches that they could have started their own watch repair shop. Kyle smiled at the memory as he thought, *Well, we could have if Dad knew how to repair watches.*

Kyle remembered clearly that as the day wore on, the sun would get so hot that they were forced to retreat to the water to cool off. Kyle would run out into the waves and dive under the water. His skin, which was turning a bright shade of pink, felt instantly relieved with the cooling effects of the water. His dad would follow close behind Kyle. Once he had immersed his body, he would swim over to play with Kyle. Kyle remembered that his dad would pick him up out of the water and launch him through the air. As Kyle neared the surface of the water he tucked his legs and arms close in to his body so he could make a gigantic splash.

Once they finished playing around in the water, they would head to the car and pull out the cooler. They had spread a blanket out under the shade of a nearby tree and pulled out their PB&J sandwiches, the chips, and their bottles of water. Dad had insisted that if they were going to be out in the sun all day they could not have soda to drink. He had said that it was an absolute necessity to hydrate their bodies as much as possible. Kyle would whine a little bit at first, but he recalled having to admit that the water hit the spot after they had been baking in the sun for hours.

It had seemed to Kyle that they had explored every square inch of that beach on those wonderful Saturdays. There was one thing, though, that had puzzled him about his dad. Although the beach was beautiful there was so much more to explore there. His dad, in spite of Kyle's persistent pleas, never wanted to go anywhere but the beach. Even now, Kyle could picture with stunning clarity the steep cliffs that lined the last quarter mile of the beach. He had conjured up all kinds of stories in his mind about what might possibly be hidden in those cliffs. In his childish imagination, he had pictured a civilization of nomads roaming about the jagged rocks. He knew he had never actually seen anyone, but he had been convinced that they were there nonetheless.

At the end of every trip, Kyle remembered that no matter how much fun he had had, and no matter what little treasures they had found, he left feeling a little empty. He never seemed to be able to shake the feeling that they were missing something *amazing*. Every time they packed up the car to go home he had assured himself that the next time they were there he would convince his dad to go with him to explore the cliffs. Yet every time they had gone his dad had said the same thing. "Kyle, there really is nothing to see there. It's nothing but a bunch of rocks. I'm not going to bring you up there only to have you fall and hurt yourself. Your mother would never forgive me if something bad happened to you." And just like that, the discussion had been over.

Although Kyle had never stopped asking to go, eventually they had run out of Saturdays. About a year and a half ago his dad had gotten a new job. The job had been good news for the family because it meant that his dad would make more money. But Kyle found himself wishing that the job offer had never come along. Now his dad's schedule for the new job meant that he worked both Saturday and Sunday every single week. Kyle hoped that someday his dad might be able to get out of working on the weekend. However, he had to deal with the reality of the way things were now.

When he had first found out about his dad's job, he had thought about asking his mom to take him to the beach. He figured that she would agree to do it every so often. Unfortunately, his mom had so many things that she had to do around the house on the weekends that he had known the trips would not be an every-weekend event. He could not fault her for that. She did have her own job that she worked at during the week. He thought about her coming home at the end of the day completely exhausted, but even still she made dinner every night and made sure Kyle had finished his homework. After careful consideration, Kyle had decided that he would not trouble his mom to take him to the beach.

Kyle had taken to walking or riding his bike on the weekends to pass the time. One of those first Saturdays that he spent without his dad, he was riding his bike around the neighborhood and had been struck with a sudden urge to go check out the beach. He had found himself pedaling rapidly through the remainder of the neighborhood and then out onto the highway that led to the beach. He and his dad had gone so often that he could have made the whole trip with his eyes closed. He remembered feeling a sense of expectation that something great was going to be revealed to him upon his arrival at the beach. When he had finally arrived, he pulled his bike into the parking lot and felt a wave of disappointment wash over him. The beach had been empty, save for a few sunbathers. He almost teared up when he thought of how much he wished he and his dad could go exploring together again.

But as fast as the tears sprang to his eyes, he had forced them away. He had vowed to himself at that very moment that dad or no dad, he was *going to* find out what mysteries were locked in those cliffs.

Ever since that day, he had made many a journey to the beach and had kept his promise to himself. He had indeed found something very, very interesting in those cliffs. He had wanted to share his discovery with his dad, but he knew he would be in serious trouble if he did. That meant that he certainly could not tell his mom. She was the biggest worry-wart he had met in his life. In addition, there was the problem of the two men he had encountered at the cliffs. Kyle wasn't sure what he would do if he ran into them again. He told himself that all he could do was try to avoid them at all costs, and that if he did run into them, he would figure out a way to get away from them.

Kyle was not sure what jogged his memory, but he suddenly remembered that Kaitlin was waiting for him. "Oh, rats!" he exclaimed. "I forgot about meeting Kaitlin outside!" He jumped out of the kitchen chair and headed toward the living room. His mom was absorbed in the sermon she was listening to, so she barely acknowledged that Kyle was standing there. After a minute, Kyle finally secured her attention. "Mom, I'm going out to the backyard. I'll probably be out there for a little while. Kaitlin is going to come hang out with me."

"Oh, OK, honey, I'll call you when it's time for lunch," his mom said.

Kyle nodded in agreement and headed toward their back door.

CHAPTER 5

Kyle's first stop outside was at the tool shed. As he approached it he noticed that the old metal shed was looking pretty dilapidated. There were spots of metallic paint that had peeled and flaked off, leaving gigantic uneven bare spots. The spots looked dark against the white paint, at least what was left of it, and it reminded him of a spotted cow. The hinges on the double doors were completely covered in rust. It made Kyle wonder how the doors were even able to open. They always did open, eventually, but he had to pull extra hard to get them to budge. The funny thing, Kyle thought, was that once they made it open more than a half inch they would swing wide and free, as if there was nothing wrong with them at all. He had learned that if he didn't get out of the way quickly, those swinging doors would clobber him.

The padlock on the latch was the only thing that seemed to be keeping would-be thieves from breaking in. Of course, Kyle mused, if they *really* wanted to break in, the rusted hinges would probably break off and they could just get in through the door that way. Kyle paused briefly in front of the doors before opening them. He recalled his dad promising him that they would replace the shed.

Kyle had been complaining about how ugly it looked and, more importantly, how hard it had become to open the doors. "I know, son," his dad had said. "I need to make a little more money to be able to afford a new shed. That's one of the reasons why I'm taking this new job. With the extra money I'll make, it won't be long before we will be out here putting up the new shed." Kyle sighed as he realized that was a year and a half ago. His dad put in a lot of long hours and, more often than not, was too tired to do much of anything around the house.

Shaking off the memories, he unlocked the doors and twisted the latch to open them. As usual, when he yanked on the doors, the doors creaked and groaned in protest and then swung wide open. Out of habit, Kyle jumped backward, but this time the door on the right side cracked him on the forehead. "OUCH!" Kyle hollered. He kicked at the dumb old door that he was sure had been out to get him. He gingerly rubbed his forehead and realized that it must be his increasing strength that had caused the doors to go flying like they did. He glared at the traitorous door. He came to the conclusion that either he was going to have to oil the hinges so he didn't have to pull so hard, or he was going to have to learn how to move faster and get out of the way.

It was a bright, sunny day outside, but the shed itself was pitch-black inside. A tiny sliver of light peeked through a crack in the roof of the structure, but that was not even close to enough light to be able to see anything with. Kyle fished a flashlight out of his left pants pocket. He pushed the button to turn it on and ran the beam along the inside front of the shed. Kyle remembered that on his last excursion he had been in a hurry to grab his gear and get going. He honestly couldn't remember if he had knocked anything over in his haste to get out of there. If he had accidentally disturbed something, and if he wasn't careful, he could unknowingly step on an upended rake. Kyle shook his head and mumbled, "No way! I've already gotten a bump on my head. No more injuries today!" Once he had scanned the dirt floor and was satisfied that there were no pitfalls waiting for him, he swept the beam to the back right corner of the shed.

Kyle's dad had cleared out this spot, shifting all of the lawn equipment from the right side to the left, and dubbed it "Kyle's Corner." After their first Saturday trip to the beach, Kyle had brought back a bucket with seashells and rocks that they had found. His dad had utterly refused to allow him to keep the bucket up in his room. He had insisted that if Kyle pulled out the rocks and shells to look at them, then the sand that covered them would fall off and get tracked all over inside the house. Kyle couldn't help but smile as he remembered the pinched, worried expression on his dad's face when he said, "Uh-uh, sorry, buddy. Your mom would have my head! Or worse yet," he said with a wink, "she might make me do the vacuuming!"

So Kyle and his dad had placed a barrel in the corner, which would be where Kyle would place his treasures. They stacked bags of fertilizer in front of the barrel to disguise it. A small stepladder was leaned up against the barrel as well. A couple of rakes were leaned up in front of the ladder to further camouflage the barrel. Once Kyle had placed his bucket inside, the two had grabbed some old beat-up burlap bags and threw them over the top of the barrel for good measure. He remembered dusting his hands off on his jeans and taking a step back to view their handiwork. His dad had also retreated back a few steps, and they had both stared at the corner in silence. To Kyle, this corner of the shed had not appeared to be any different from any other part of the shed. It seemed, as he had looked at the shed from one end to the other, that it was no different from any other shed they could find on any of their neighbors' properties. Kyle's dad had gotten a big grin, rubbed his hand over the top of Kyle's head in a loving gesture, and asked, "Satisfied, kiddo?" Kyle had beamed up at his dad and almost screeched the words, "It's PERFECT!"

Up until that day, Kyle could not remember his dad caring about locking up the shed. He had always said that their lawn mower and rakes were as old as he was, and that if someone really wanted them *that bad* they could have them. Kyle remembered watching the expression change on his dad's face in a matter of moments. Kyle hadn't been sure what that look meant at first, but he remembered clearly how quickly his dad disappeared out of the shed. Kyle hadn't thought much about it because he was still marveling at his corner. A few minutes later his dad had reappeared with a padlock and handed it to Kyle. "Here you go, son," he had said. "You'll have to learn the combination, but that should keep your finds safe and sound." "Aw, Dad, you're the best!" Kyle had exclaimed.

He had immediately studied the sticker on the back of the lock, and after repeating the combination to himself five times, he had had it committed to memory. He had turned the dial to the right, to the left, and then to the right again. He remembered hearing the click as the tumbler fell into place and the lock popped open. He had repeated the process several times just to be sure he truly had the combination memorized. Once he was satisfied, he had put the padlock on the latch and clicked the lock shut. Later that night, before going to sleep, he had recited the combination over and over to himself until he had fallen asleep. He had never had a problem recalling the numbers since then.

Now Kyle's gaze followed the beam of light to the back corner. The memories were good, but he felt a wave of sadness that accompanied them. He sure did miss his time with his dad. He sighed heavily, and his shoulders heaved with the weight. *Well,* he thought to himself and sighed, *I can't change that Dad has to work weekends.* He sighed once more, and then resigned himself to staying focused on the present. "Right now," he told himself, "I've got to find that box."

The box he was thinking of was actually a small treasure chest that had a lock of its own. Kyle's mom had surprised him with it about a year after he and his dad had started taking their Saturday trips to the beach. Kyle had never really told her much about their trips, but apparently his dad had. Their finds had become much more diverse than rocks and shells. Although Kyle still enjoyed rummaging through them and admiring each one for its beauty, the things he wanted to protect now were items like the watches, the coins, some unique rings, and the key.

Kyle reached the bags of fertilizer and removed two from the top of the pile. He then lifted the burlap bags from the top of the barrel and leaned over it. The barrel appeared to be about three-fourths full of rocks. Kyle reached in with both hands and began scooping up rocks and setting them on top of the burlap bags. He repeated the process until he was about three inches down into the barrel and he could finally see the curved top of the treasure chest. He was unable to get his hands around the sides of it to be able to hoist it out of the barrel. "Doggone it!" he fumed. "I hid this thing much too well!" He continued to dig rocks away from the sides of the chest, but other rocks slid into the place of the ones he had removed. He huffed in frustration and said, "I'm going to have to figure out another way to do this. This is way too much work!"

Finally, he had made enough headway to get his hands around the sides of the chest and was able to dig in underneath it. Each rock was about the size of a golf ball. Their size left him barely enough room to get a grip and have any leverage. In spite of this setback, Kyle was determined and he somehow managed to pull the chest out. He stared at the chest for a few brief moments and then set it down. Around his neck was a string that he had fashioned into a makeshift necklace. He fingered the key that hid under his shirt and pulled it up into the light. He removed the string from around his neck and looped it around his wrist. Then he picked up the chest and proceeded toward the doors of the shed.

Kyle could tell that it was getting close to one o'clock by the position of the sun. As he approached the opening, it was shining fiercely and intently right into his eyes. The sun was blinding him, and Kyle decided that it would be wise to stretch his foot out in front of him and feel around to keep himself from tripping over the threshold of the shed. His left foot skidded along the dirt floor until it made contact with the front wall. Once he was sure he was in a safe position, he lifted his right foot up and over the threshold. He took a step out onto the ground and lifted his left foot to step completely outside. As he did this, he turned around to swing one of the shed doors closed. He then bent down to set the chest on the ground. His next maneuver was to close the second shed door, and, as he did so, he stepped back to get out of the path of the door. He felt something beneath his left foot that didn't feel like grass or dirt.

"Owwww!" he heard a female voice howl.

Kyle turned to see Kaitlin hopping up and down on one foot and holding the other one with both hands. Her eyes had tears forming in them, and Kyle was instantly horrified when he realized that it was her foot that he had stepped on. *Oh boy*, he thought, *I've really done it now! She's going to be* hopping *mad at me!* The little pun he had made and the sight of her bouncing up and down proved to be too much for him. He could not stop himself from fits of laughter at the scene before him.

Kaitlin, who was still holding her foot in one hand, swatted at him with the other. "Kyle, you're mean! You squashed me with that big clown shoe of yours and now you're laughing at me!"

Kyle, who was finally now able to catch his breath between bouts of laughter, choked out, "Kaitlin, I'm so sorry! I had no idea you were there. I was so confused because I knew the ground felt funny, but by the time I figured it out, there you were, hopping up and down. Then I had the thought in my head that you would be 'hopping mad' at me, and I couldn't stop myself from laughing!"

Kaitlin swatted at him one more time and said, "It's not funny, Kyle. That really hurt!" But then as she thought of what she must have looked like to him, she began to crack the tiniest little smile.

She noticed the treasure chest on the ground next to the shed. "What's that?" she asked.

"We'll get to that in a minute," he responded. "But first, let me get this closed up."

He stepped around to the outside of the shed door and began to swing it shut. As he was in mid-motion Kaitlin stopped him again and turned him to face her. She examined his forehead for a minute and pointed at the bruise that was rapidly growing larger and darker. "Kyle, how on earth did this happen?" Kyle reached up to touch the spot and winced as he did. "Well," Kaitlin said, "I guess we both got injured today. What did you do to get this hideous bump on your head?"

Kyle looked at her and replied with a wink and a smile, "Oh, that? I just got into a fight with a door."

CHAPTER 6

K yle picked the chest up from the ground and walked around
to the side of the shed. A wooden fence ran around the
perimeter of the backyard. Kyle glanced up at the fence and
thought about how thankful he was that his dad had not put in one
of those short fences that you could still see over. Kyle was about
five feet tall. The fence stood at least two and a half feet taller than
he was and based on that knowledge, he approximated that the
fence was about seven and a half to eight feet high. The slats of the
boards had very little space between them, which allowed for
maximum privacy.

He motioned for Kaitlin to follow him to the side of the shed.
She followed him to the spot where he stood and watched as he
surveyed the area. He said nothing further to her, but she could see
that he was listening intently for something. What it was, she had
no idea. *He sure has been acting strange lately!* she thought. Kyle stood
motionless for what seemed like an eternity, just watching and
listening.

Finally, Kaitlin could take the suspense no longer. She interrupted his thoughts with the question, "Kyle Marshall, what on earth is going on with you? You are acting SO WEIRD!"

That last statement shook Kyle out of his trancelike state and his eyes locked onto hers. "I know you must think I've gone off the deep end, Kaitlin," he said and then sighed. "There is just so much to tell you, but I have to make sure that no one, and I mean NO ONE, ever hears what I'm about to tell you!"

Kaitlin eyed him suspiciously and said, "It can't be *that* big of a deal, Kyle. Does it have something to do with those men that we saw at church last night?" Kyle's startled reaction told Kaitlin that she was on to something.

"Yes, but SHHH!!" he said. "Here, sit down on the ground with me and let me show you something."

Kaitlin followed Kyle's lead and sat down on the green grass. There was plenty of shade where they sat because the shed was blocking the sun. The weather had been extremely warm and humid for the last week, so the coolness of the shade was a welcome relief. Kaitlin watched as Kyle loosened the string that was looped around his wrist and pulled it off with a tug. She noticed there was a key secured on the string. As she looked from the key to the chest, she realized that the key must be for the chest that Kyle seemed to be guarding with his life.

Kyle took the key in his hand and slowly slid it into the lock on the chest. He turned the key to the left and Kaitlin heard a faint click. Once Kyle removed the key from the lock, he lifted the lid and let it fall open onto the ground. The chest wasn't that large, but

Kaitlin could tell that it was made of very solid wood by the "thump" that reverberated off of the ground.

She leaned over to peek inside and saw that the chest was lined with a shiny, red satin material around the sides and under the lid. If her assumption was correct, the whole chest was probably lined with the same material, but right now she couldn't see the bottom. There seemed to be layers and layers of wadded up Kleenex. *Yuck,* she thought. *I sure hope that Kyle hasn't been blowing his nose in those tissues!*

Kyle, meanwhile, was completely oblivious to Kaitlin's facial expressions. Had he looked up at her at that very moment, he would have caught the look of disgust on her face and would have fallen over laughing. However, Kyle's only focus at that time was the objects that he would soon retrieve from the folds of tissue.

Kaitlin watched as he pulled out wads of the Kleenex and pulled out a very small plastic bag. It had a zipper closure at the top, and Kyle began to open it. As she watched, Kaitlin surveyed the bag to see if she could determine what the contents were. She realized that she couldn't really see *anything* in the bag except for what appeared to be a piece of off-white plastic. "Kyle, why are you hiding a piece of plastic in your treasure chest?" she asked. "I'm starting to think you've lost your marbles."

"Oh, for Pete's sake!" Kyle exclaimed. "Why would you think I would go to so much trouble to save a dumb old piece of plastic? Here," he said and paused while he rummaged around inside of the bag.

His fingers grasped at the small object, and he pulled it gently from the bag and said, "Hold out your hand."

Kaitlin uncurled her fingers and turned her hand with the palm facing the sky. She watched as Kyle gripped the small object between his pointer finger and his thumb and reached over to her outstretched hand. She didn't want to look at it immediately until she could get a better view of it. Kyle's hand was still hovering over the thing as if he felt like he would have to snatch it back at any second.

"Kyle, how am I supposed to see this thing if you don't move your big paw?" she asked.

Kyle grinned sheepishly and, ever so slowly, pulled his hand away from hers. Before she looked at the object in her hand, Kaitlin tried to guess what it was by how it felt. It seemed to have an odd and irregular shape. One part of it felt smooth, but on the opposite end it felt distinctly rough. It became obvious to her that she wasn't going to guess what it was by how it felt, so she stole a glance at the white thing. When she finally got a good look at it and realized what it was, her eyes squinted and her mouth twisted and contorted into a very peculiar expression. She looked at the object and then looked at Kyle. Then she looked at the white thing again and back to Kyle. Her hand started to tremble, and she almost dropped the thing in the process. Kyle, who was completely surprised by her reaction, had to move quickly before she dropped it in the grass. He lunged for her hand and rescued his precious find just before it went flying.

"Kaitlin, what are you so—" was all that Kyle was able to get out of his mouth before Kaitlin shrieked, "*EWWWWWW! Kyle, that is SO GROSS!*"

Poor Kyle was so stunned that at first he didn't know how to respond. After he recovered slightly, he attempted to soothe her by saying, "Gee whiz, Kaitlin, it's only a—"

But before he could finish his thought she interrupted with an excited, "*IT'S A TOOTH, Kyle! Oh, ICK!*" Then she scrubbed the palm of her hand on her jeans. She shuddered and shook her hand violently as if trying to remove the remnants of the germs.

Kyle's eyes were huge as he watched her reaction. "Oh my gosh, you are such a *GIRL!*" he exclaimed. "It's not like I handed you a slimy worm!"

"Well, you might as well have!" Kaitlin retorted. Then she followed that with, "Whose tooth is that anyway? Please tell me that it's yours. Then it wouldn't seem so disgusting. Oh, but it can't be. That thing is WAY too big to be yours! Is it from some kind of animal?"

Kyle tried his best to understand her rambling, and finally, he was able to make enough sense out of the jumbled words to figure out that she was asking where the tooth came from.

"Whoa! Slow down just for a minute," Kyle said, shaking his head. "In answer to one of your questions, no, it is not from an animal. Well, I guess maybe it *could be*, but I really don't think it is. It looks too much like the tooth of a human. And no, it is not my tooth. You were right, this is way too big to be my tooth." To emphasize his point, Kyle opened his mouth wide for her to look into. He poked his finger into his mouth and pointed his finger toward his largest molar. "Shee," he mumbled, "ith at leatht twith the sizhe of thith one."

Kaitlin giggled as she investigated the recesses of his mouth. She could barely understand his garbled words, but as she gazed at his molar she figured out what he was trying to tell her.

"So, where did it come from then?" she asked.

"Well, do you remember that I told you I was going to have to show you something?" he asked. Kaitlin nodded, and Kyle continued, saying, "This is only a very small part of what I have to show you. We'll actually have to *go* to this place. I can see by the look on your face that you have a whole bunch of questions that you want answered, and we will get to that. But before I do, I have one more thing in this chest that you have to see."

Kaitlin was about to say something, but then thought better of it. "OK, I'm game," she announced. "Give it your best shot. For your sake, it better not be another tooth!"

Kyle smirked and said, "I promise, it's not another tooth. Give me just a minute to get this thing out of here." With that he turned his attention to the chest once more and started pulling more tissues from it. In a flourish, he produced another plastic bag with a zipper. Kaitlin tried to get a peek at the contents, but Kyle put the bag behind his back.

"Kaitlin, are you *absolutely positive* that you want to see what is in this bag?" he teased. "After all, I wouldn't want you to get grossed out again."

"Oh, WHATEVER!!" Kaitlin huffed. She turned around as if she were going to get up and walk away and Kyle decided maybe it wasn't such a good idea to keep teasing her this way.

"I was just kidding," he said in a soothing voice. "Here," he said, bringing the bag toward her. "Hold out your hand and close your eyes."

"Kyle . . ." Kaitlin said in a warning voice.

"No, really," he assured her, "it's nothing to be afraid of."

"Well, OK then," she said and placed her upturned hand in front of him. She closed her eyes almost all the way, but Kyle caught her trying to peek.

"If you want to see, you have to follow the rules," Kyle taunted.

"Fine!" Kaitlin said and squeezed her eyes shut.

Kaitlin felt something drop into her hand that was quite a bit heavier than the tooth. She could tell that it was made out of some dense material. It seemed to her that it felt a little cold. And very rough. She ran the fingers of her other hand over the length of the object and guessed that it was approximately two inches in length. It was about half an inch wide in some areas, but then as she felt along with her fingertips, she noticed that the object got slightly wider. The shape was foreign to her, but it felt as if one end had some curves. Three of them. Well, at least she thought there were three. She ran her fingers down to the other end of the object and noticed that it seemed to have two spots protruding from the side. By now she was completely confused. Kyle called it "confuzzled."

What a funny word, she thought now. But it did fit. "OK, Kyle, I give. What is it?" she asked.

"Open your eyes and see for yourself," he said with amusement. "Wait. No, first guess what you think it is."

"Um, some kind of dog treat?" she suggested.

Kyle snickered and said, "Not even close! Do you give up?"

"Yes, Kyle, I give up," she said. Then she sighed and said in a defeated voice, "Now, can I please see it?"

Kyle tweaked her on the nose, which made Kaitlin almost drop whatever it was in her hand. "Oops, sorry," he said, but he didn't really sound like he was sorry at all. "Go ahead."

Kaitlin's first glimpse of the thing told her that it was made out of some kind of rock. Its texture was slightly rough, as she had deduced while she was holding it. It looked like it had been severely weathered. Upon closer inspection, she noticed the curved areas that she had felt earlier. There were indeed three curves, each joined to the other, with the one in the middle being higher than the two on either side. Her eyes traveled the length of the object and she noticed that there were two rectangular-shaped pieces jutting off of what appeared to be a narrow barrel.

Suddenly, a look crossed her face and Kyle smiled to himself. *Yep,* he thought, *she's got it figured out.*

"Kyle..." she said slowly, "is this what I think it is? Is it a... key?"

Kyle jumped up and danced a little jig. "Ding, ding, ding!" he exclaimed. "What do we have for our winner, Drew?"

"Oh, you're a regular riot, Kyle Marshall!" Kaitlin sputtered. "I know darn well this is not a key for a brand new car."

"Right again!" Kyle said and grinned from ear to ear.

"Well, then, *what is it for?*" she asked in a pleading voice.

Kyle scratched his head and tried to figure out how to best answer that. In the end, he shrugged his shoulders and replied, "Honestly, I haven't figured that out yet. But I did find the tooth and the key in the same place. I think they are tied together somehow."

"Kyle, what are you talking about? How can a tooth and a key possibly have anything to do with one another?" Kaitlin asked.

"I really don't know, Kaitlin," he said with a sigh, "but I do believe in my heart that somehow they are connected. Listen, I know I need to explain more to you, but how about we plan on taking a little trip after school tomorrow? Are you game?"

"Sure, Kyle," she responded, "but . . . am I going to get in trouble for this?"

"Not that I'm aware of," he answered.

Just then, Kyle's mom came to the back door of the house and called out, "Kyle, Kaitlin, lunch is ready. You two come in here and wash up."

"OK, Mom, be right there," he said loudly enough for the whole neighborhood to hear. He didn't want her to come looking for them. So far, Kaitlin was the only one who knew about the tooth and the key.

"We better get in there, Kaitlin, or Mom will come looking for us," he said hurriedly. "We better put this stuff back in the shed for now."

The two of them tossed the items back into their bags, threw the tissues back over them, locked the chest, and put it back into the barrel.

"Don't worry about the rocks for now," Kyle said, looking at the chest. "We'll just throw the burlap bags over the barrel." Just then, Kyle heard Kaitlin's stomach growl.

"Kyle," Kaitlin said as she took off like lightning toward the door, "if you don't hurry up I'm going to eat every last little bite of that lunch. I'm *so hungry!*"

CHAPTER 7

Once they had finished eating their lunch, Kyle got up, flung open the back door, and stepped out into the yard. After walking a distance, he turned and looked over his shoulder to see if Kaitlin was following him. To his dismay, he saw her still perched on her chair at the kitchen table. His mom was in the process of clearing away the leftover food off the table. Kaitlin, it appeared, was not quite full. She was grabbing another half of a sandwich and shoving it into her mouth. She swallowed it quickly, grabbed another one, and stuffed it into her mouth. He wondered if she was chewing it or if she was inhaling it. *Gee whiz*, he thought, *and they say boys eat a lot!*

His mom seemed to be stifling her laughter. Kyle heard her tell Kaitlin, "Honey, if you're still hungry I can make more."

"Oh, no, thath OK, Mittheth Marthall. I've had enough," Kaitlin said with her cheeks still stuffed full of sandwich.

Kyle's mom smiled and handed her a bag of potato chips and said, "You can take these outside with you. It looks like Kyle is not-so-patiently waiting on you."

Kyle winked at his mom and said, "I'm glad you stopped her, Mom. If she would have eaten any more we may have needed a forklift to get her out of that chair."

That was all it took. Kaitlin was up and running full speed out the door and toward Kyle. She caught up to him in the middle of the backyard, and she stood next to him, still chewing the remnants of her sandwich. In her left hand, she was carrying the bag of chips, but with her free right hand she socked Kyle in the arm.

"Ow!" Kyle yelped. "What was that for?"

Kaitlin's eyes turned to blazes of fire and she fumed, "You know exactly what that was for! That comment about the forklift!"

Kyle rubbed his arm and winced. He looked her in the eyes and with the greatest sincerity said, "I was just trying to get you mad enough to get you out of that chair. It worked, didn't it? By the way, you've got a mean right hook!"

Kaitlin shrugged and said nonchalantly, "What can I say . . . I have an older brother."

Kyle looked at her free hand and said, "Remind me never to make you mad again."

Just as they turned and started toward the shed, they heard some loud noises coming from inside of it. A startled Kyle froze in mid-step. He stood there ever so quietly, listening. They heard the sound of some object being tossed and crashing into another object.

"What the heck?" Kyle shouted, and he took off running.

Kaitlin could hear more thumps and could tell that some of the garden tools were being carelessly heaved to the ground. Her level of fear was so great that for a few moments, she did not move a muscle and couldn't even speak.

In her own backyard, Chester, her beloved little pet, had been calmly wandering around and sniffing at every plant, tree, rock, or garden hose that he came into contact with. He had found a rabbit hiding in a row of lilies and began barking up a storm. The scared little rabbit had taken off, running for his life, and Chester was running as fast as his little legs would allow him to keep up. The incessant barking and yipping was nothing new to Kaitlin. She had learned to tune it out.

As she stood there in Kyle's backyard, watching Kyle as he approached the doors of the shed, she barely registered what was going on in front of her. The invader, it seemed, had not anticipated the ruckus, because the noise in the shed stopped suddenly. Kaitlin watched as Kyle crept stealthily toward the shed.

"Kyle, don't go in there! Please!" she said quietly, but fervently. "It's not safe!"

Kyle turned around and she saw a frightened but determined look on his face. He motioned to the doors and then put his finger up in front of his pursed lips as a warning for her to be quiet. He swiveled back toward the shed and reached out his hand to grab the handle of the door on the right side.

Oh no, Kaitlin thought, *that's the squeaky door!* She had a picture in her mind of Kyle opening the door and the robber, or whoever he was, coming out and clobbering Kyle.

In the meantime, Chester began his pursuit of the rabbit again and started to bark up a storm. Apparently, Chester's barking had startled the would-be thief, and he flung the shed door wide open. Kyle, who had approached the shed to see what was going on, was right in the path of the door. Poor Kyle received the second blow to his forehead that day. Kaitlin watched as he collapsed on the ground in a heap. In a flash, a man ran out of the shed, around the side, and then behind it. In that brief moment that she had seen him, she had noticed that he had very dark hair. He had a ski mask on, but some tufts of his hair peeked out of the large hole for his eyes. He was dressed in a black sweatshirt and pants and wore black shoes.

Kaitlin stood, watching intently to see what the intruder would do. From her vantage point she was sure to get a better view of him once he finally walked out from behind the shed.

The would-be thief took off running. It seemed to Kaitlin that it only took a split second for him to reach the gate. She watched in shock as he swung a large metal wrench at the lever that was holding the gate closed. She heard a loud ringing noise as the two metals clashed, and suddenly the gate sprung open. The man lunged through the gate and sprinted around the house until he was out of sight.

Kaitlin, who was in a state of shock, was not sure that she could move her feet. She knew she needed to go check on Kyle and make sure he was OK. "Come on, girl!" she chided herself. "The big nasty man is gone." Slowly, ever so slowly, she began to make her way toward where Kyle lay unconscious on the ground. With each step, she felt the paralyzing fear begin to melt away. She broke into a run and soon she was standing over Kyle's motionless body.

"Kyle! Are y . . . y . . . you . . . OK?" she stammered. There was no response from Kyle, so she crouched down and began to do the only thing she knew to do. She grasped both sides of his body with her hands and shook the living daylights out of him.

Kyle groaned, and she saw his arm begin to move. She watched as, almost involuntarily, he lifted his hand up to his forehead and began rubbing it over the goose egg that had appeared after his first run-in with the shed door.

"Oh man, that smarts!" she heard Kyle exclaim in a weak voice. He began to sit up and look around as if in a daze. Then she saw his eyes focus and she noticed that his face had contorted as if he were straining to recall why he was on the ground. While Kaitlin continued to watch him, Kyle's eyes grew wide, and it appeared that the events of the last few minutes were coming back to him.

"Kaitlin," he asked, "where is he? Is he still in there?"

She began to shake her head no but then realized that his eyes were fixed on the shed and not on her. "No, he's not," she replied.

"Well, what happened?" he hissed. "Where did he go?"

"I'm not exactly sure *where* he is," she answered. "Chester started barking at a rabbit in my yard and it must have scared the guy. He threw the door open just as you were reaching for it and it conked you on the head. You were knocked out cold. He ran behind the shed and hid again for about a minute, but then Chester started barking again. I saw him running toward the gate, and he had some kind of tool in his hand. The next thing I knew he was hitting the latch on the gate with the tool and the gate opened. The last thing I saw was him running around the side of your house and into your front yard."

"Did you see him? Could you tell what he looked like?" Kyle asked.

"Ummm . . . well," Kaitlin said, then paused and began again, "I didn't really see *him*. I saw what he was wearing. He had a black ski mask on and black sweatpants and a sweatshirt. She paused and said, "Now that I think about it, his shoes were black too."

Kyle sighed heavily, and it was obviously a sigh of frustration.

Kaitlin continued, "I *did* see his hair though. It was very dark brown, almost black."

Kyle, who was thoroughly confused, asked, "Wait. How could you know what color hair he has? I thought he was wearing a ski mask."

"He was," Kaitlin said, "but I could see some of his hair poking out through his eye hole."

"Oh," was all Kyle could manage. He slowly stood up and surveyed the entrance to the shed. Without turning his body, he asked Kaitlin, "You said that you saw him carrying some kind of tool, right? Did you see him holding anything else in his hands?"

Kaitlin hesitated only for a moment before she replied, "No, I'm sure of it. He didn't have anything else. I think he was holding a wrench."

"What about my mom?" Kyle asked. "Did she notice anything that happened?"

"I don't think so," Kaitlin replied. "I'm sure she's in there watching her television show with the volume turned way up. You know how she is. Besides, Chester was barking so loud that I don't know how she could possibly have heard anything over that noise!"

Kyle smiled, but then his face froze. "Awww man," he said, "he could have put something in his pockets. Sweatpants have pockets sometimes. I need to get in there and make sure he didn't find my chest!"

He was in the shed in a flash, and Kaitlin followed him inside. As they looked around, and their eyes adjusted to the darkness, they could see that there was a big pile of tools and lawn bags lying scattered all over the floor. Rakes and hoes had been knocked over in the man's haste to get out the door. The lawn mower had been moved and so had the leaf blower. But they were still in the corner of the shed.

As they both looked in that direction, Kyle half-smiled and said jokingly, "Well, I guess he wasn't here to steal the lawn mower. Dad will be disappointed. He wanted an excuse to get a new one."

Kaitlin chuckled and then said with some urgency, "Kyle, what about the chest? Shouldn't we make sure it's still there?"

Kyle didn't bother to respond but headed immediately for the barrel. Surprisingly enough, the burlap sacks were still draped over the top of it. Kyle ripped them off the top of the barrel and flung them aside. He peeked inside, and with a muffled voice he told Kaitlin, "It's still here. But I have to check and make sure the tooth and the key are still inside."

Kaitlin waited for a response from him. Even though she had no idea why Kyle insisted they were so important, she would feel just awful if they were gone. She could hear Kyle grunting as he leaned over the barrel. He was massaging his sore forehead with one hand and rapidly removing tissues with the other.

"Oh, thank God!" she heard him exclaim. He pulled out the two bags and held them up for her to see. With the darkness surrounding her, it was hard to make out whether the objects were still in those bags. But she knew that if they had been empty Kyle would not still be standing here. Instead, he would be tearing out of the backyard and searching high and low until he found the man with his treasures.

Kyle carefully placed the bags and the tissues back into the chest and locked it with his key. He turned to Kaitlin and said, "I don't know where I'm going to hide this thing, but obviously, it's not safe here. And I can't sneak it up to my room. Mom would see it and she would demand that it went back in the shed. Oh, rats! What am I going to do?"

Kaitlin pondered for a moment, and then she answered, "I know you may not like this idea, but how about if we bring it over to my house? We could hide it in *my* shed. That man would never dream of looking for it in there. Besides, with Chester in the backyard, he couldn't get anywhere close to the shed."

Kyle was about to say, "No way! It needs to stay here!" but then he thought better of it. She was right, after all. Chester's incessant barking would be the perfect deterrent to a would-be burglar. "I guess," he said and shrugged his shoulders.

"Oh, Kyle," Kaitlin said in a soothing voice, "I know you want to have your chest here, but I promise that my little ol' Chester will keep it safe."

He finally agreed, and they carried the chest out into the light of the backyard. Kyle heard Chester's incessant barking and laughed. Chester was at it again, he thought. That poor rabbit didn't know what he had been in for when he hopped into Kaitlin's yard. *I bet he'll never do that again!* Kyle thought. For some odd reason, the thought of Chester scaring the rabbit away gave him peace that no one would be able to get anywhere near the chest.

He and Kaitlin started walking over to the side of the fence that bordered Kaitlin's yard. Through the narrow gaps in the fence, Kyle and Kaitlin watched Chester as he chased a rabbit, his little legs working with all their might.

"Chester, here boy," Kaitlin called out to him. The little dog abruptly stopped chasing the rabbit and turned sharply to run up to Kaitlin and Kyle.

Once Chester stopped directly on the other side of the fence, Kyle crouched down and spoke softly to the dog. "Thank you, Chester. If it wasn't for you that man would have found my treasure. You're a good little guy." In response Chester said, "Arf," and Kyle and Kaitlin giggled. "You were right, Kaitlin. I have nothing to worry about. Let's go put this chest in your shed and then I'll tell you about that man."

CHAPTER 8

The two friends walked to the back door of Kyle's house. Kyle was holding the chest in his hands. "Kaitlin, we have to tell Mom that we are going over to your house. Can you please open the door? I'll just stand here and tell her what we're doing," he said.

"No problem," Kaitlin answered as she reached for the doorknob. With a twist of the knob, the door squeaked, and it popped open. Kyle heard the TV blaring in the background and realized that Kaitlin had been right. His mom had heard nothing that had happened outside. Kaitlin looked at him with a smile and a gleam in her eyes as if she was saying, "I told you so." Kyle nodded, indicating to her that he understood, and that, yes, she had indeed been right.

"Mom . . ." Kyle called out. Kyle heard the volume of the TV being turned down.

"Yes, honey, what is it?" she asked.

He responded, "We're going next door to Kaitlin's house for a little bit."

"OK, honey, but how long do you think you'll be gone? I have to run to the store. I only have to get a few things, but I wanted to make sure that you don't need me for anything before I leave," his mom said.

"Well," Kyle said, and thought for a minute before he answered, "it won't be more than an hour. I still have homework to finish before school tomorrow."

Oh, good," his mom said. "I'll be back from the store by then. Speaking of food, Kaitlin, are you sure you got enough to eat? I can send some sandwiches home with you."

Kaitlin looked as if she wanted to dive in through the back door and scoop up more of the sandwiches, but Kyle gave her a look that stopped her in her tracks. "Uh, no, that's OK, Mrs. Marshall," she said with the sound of defeat in her voice. "I had enough already."

"You sure did!" Kyle said, poking fun at her. "You ate enough for both of us!" Kaitlin swatted at Kyle, but because he held the chest in his hands, he couldn't defend himself. "All right, truce!" he said and laughed. Kyle addressed his mom once more, "We're going next door now. See you in a little bit."

"Bye, Mrs. Marshall," Kaitlin chimed in, and then she closed the back door.

Kyle led the way to the gate in the fence and when he saw the broken latch he realized that he was going to have some explaining to do to his dad later. *How on earth am I going to explain this away?* Kyle thought to himself. Kaitlin saw the look on his face and opened her mouth like she was about to say something, but Kyle stopped her. "I'll figure it out later," he said. "Right now, I just want to get this thing hidden in your shed." With one hand, he reached up and rubbed the bump on his forehead and then he groaned and mumbled, "Boy, I'm never going to hear the end of this one at school tomorrow. When the guys hear that I got smacked in the head with the shed door they'll be laughing at me all day. No, make that all week," he finished and groaned again.

Kaitlin looked at him sympathetically and said, "I'll tell them it was my fault, that I'm a big klutz."

"Nah, thanks anyway, Kaitlin," Kyle answered. "That wouldn't stop them from teasing me anyway. They would probably tease me more and say that I let a girl beat me up."

"Boys are so stu—" Kaitlin began, but then caught herself. She looked at Kyle sheepishly and started again. "What I meant to say is that most boys are, well, you know. But not you."

"Good save," Kyle teased.

Kaitlin turned red in the face and huffed, "Kyle Marshall, if you were like them I would not be friends with you!"

"That's good to know," Kyle said and winked at her. "All right, let's get this thing next door."

They walked around the front of Kyle's house and Kaitlin had a momentary flashback of watching the intruder running in this same direction. Her eyes darted back and forth, scanning the area to make sure he wasn't hiding somewhere, waiting to jump out at them.

Kyle noticed her reaction and said, "I sure wish I knew where he ran off to."

"Me too," Kaitlin agreed. They proceeded cautiously, still a little worried that the man was lurking behind some bush or tree. "Kyle, that man had dark hair," Kaitlin began. "Was he one of the men that we saw at church last night?"

Kyle didn't answer right away, but he knew that Kaitlin was very perceptive, and he should have known she would put two and two together.

"Well, I obviously didn't get a good look at him, or *any* look at him, for that matter," he said. "But yes, I believe it was him. Who else would be snooping around in my shed?"

Kaitlin was quick to respond, "Well, he sure wasn't there to steal the lawn mower, so that rules out some random robber. But Kyle, why was *that* man in your shed? How would *he* know that you have that big ugly tooth and that key?"

Kyle opened his mouth to give her an explanation, but then thought better of it. "Let's get this hidden away first, just in case he decides to come back. Then I'll explain the whole thing." Kaitlin's face scrunched up and he could tell that she was not happy at all, but then she started walking across her driveway toward her backyard. *Uh-oh*, Kyle thought, *she's way too quiet. That's never a good sign.*

Kaitlin proceeded to the gate without a sound, opened it, and led the way to the shed. Kyle followed her, wishing that it had never come to this. He wanted his chest and its treasures safe and sound at home where they belonged. But that was the whole problem; they were no longer safe there. That man could come back anytime snooping around, only this time he was sure to be a little smarter about it. When he came back, Kyle was certain that he would do so under cover of night. He was also certain that he would make sure that Chester was inside the house before he made another attempt.

As if he knew that Kyle was thinking about him, Chester came bounding up to Kyle and started running circles around his legs. Kyle nearly tripped over him, but he caught himself before he and the chest both took a tumble. Kyle stopped briefly and squatted down to pat the little dog on the head. "You're a good boy, Chester," he said as he scratched behind the dog's ears. "You're going to have to be extra alert, OK, buddy?" He pointed at the chest he was holding and said, "Guard this with your life!" The dog looked at him, not as if he understood, but as if he just wanted this attention to go on forever. Kyle chuckled and said, "Well, it's a good thing there are a lot of rabbits out this time of year."

Kyle finally reached the shed, where Kaitlin stood impatiently waiting for him. She placed a key in the U-shaped lock and turned it until it opened with a click. She opened the door and made way for Kyle to precede her. As Kyle stepped into the darkness, he saw a flash of movement on the ground in front of him. Just at that moment, Chester barked furiously, his little body bouncing up and down with excitement. Until now, Kyle hadn't even noticed that he had given a startled yelp. Kaitlin, who was standing next to him, saw the ashen color of his face and doubled over laughing.

Kyle could feel his hands trembling and felt as if he could drop the chest. "What . . . was . . . *THAT*?" Kyle finally managed to get out.

Kaitlin was laughing so hysterically at his reaction that she could hardly breathe. When the laughter finally subsided, at least temporarily, she reprimanded him with the comment, "You big chicken! That was just Marvin."

"Marvin?" an astonished Kyle asked. "Who, or what, is Marvin?"

"He's a mouse, goofy!" she said, beginning to giggle again. "He's not going to hurt you. He's just a teeny tiny little thing. We found him hiding out in here over the winter. The poor thing looked so hungry that my dad went inside and got him a piece of bread and some water. I fell in love with the little guy—couldn't help it with that cute little face of his. So, every day I bring out some cheese or some little tidbit for him to eat. I guess I've kind of adopted him."

Kyle shuddered and stepped back a bit, as if he were hesitant to go any further. "I don't like mice," was all he said.

"Well, I don't like big ugly teeth, but I held your precious tooth," Kaitlin teased.

"Yeah," Kyle agreed, "but you didn't know what it was before it was in your hand. This," he said and shuddered again, "I already know what it is . . . and I don't like it!"

Kaitlin tapped the back of Kyle's heel with the toe of her shoe, as if to prod him into moving. "Come on, you big baby, get in there. If you think the guys are going to tease you over that bump, just wait 'til I tell them about what I just witnessed. I can just hear them razzing you now . . ." Kaitlin trailed off as she burst into another fit of laughter.

"You wouldn't dare!" Kyle seethed.

"Oh, brother! Kyle, you ought to know that I would never say anything to them. After all, I wouldn't want you to lose your manly reputation!" Kaitlin said with a hint of sarcasm in her voice. "You better get used to Marvin, Kyle, if you're going to keep your chest in here." In a final jabbing gesture, she added, "You're going to be seeing a lot of him!"

"Oh, rats!" Kyle exclaimed, and Kaitlin burst out laughing all over again.

Kyle stole a glance into the shed once more, and when he was satisfied that he didn't see any movement, he finally stepped inside. The two of them rummaged through the shed to find a good hiding spot. Kaitlin's dad had a humongous rollaway toolbox. It was bright red and had lots of drawers in the top half of it. Kyle quickly determined that those drawers would not be deep enough for the chest to fit inside and still close the drawer. However, he noticed that the bottom of the toolbox had a large cabinet with two metal doors. He figured Kaitlin's dad must store his large power tools in there.

"Kaitlin, do you think your dad would mind if I hid the chest in here?" he asked as he pointed at the doors.

"Oh, I'm pretty sure he wouldn't mind," Kaitlin said with a knowing smile. "I can't remember the last time he used any of the tools in there. I think those are just more for show; or maybe just in case he ever needed to fix something. But my dad doesn't fix anything around the house. He always hires someone to do the work for him."

Kyle smiled with satisfaction. To him there could not be a more perfect hiding spot. *Well,* he thought to himself, *at least as perfect as it can be here.*

Kyle bent over to open the door on the toolbox and got a very unpleasant surprise. Little Marvin bounded out of the storage cabinet and ran across Kyle's feet.

Kaitlin looked at Kyle's face and saw that it was as white as a sheet. She laughed until she had tears streaming out of her eyes, but finally managed to tease Kyle, saying, "Well, it looks like Marvin thought that was a good hiding spot too."

Kyle, who still looked stricken, said, "Very funny, Kaitlin!"

"Oh, for Pete's sake, Kyle!" Kaitlin chided him. "Just put your chest in there and we'll lock this shed back up. You'll get used to Marvin eventually, whether you like it or not." Kyle shoved the chest in and closed the cabinet door. He and Kaitlin retreated out of the shed and she locked it up once again. "See?" she said. "All safe and sound."

"Yeah, as long as Marvin doesn't chew through the wood," Kyle retorted.

"It will be fine," Kaitlin assured him. "Now tell me about those two men."

"OK," Kyle said slowly. "I really don't have much time now because I have to get home and finish my homework." Kyle saw a warning look flash in Kaitlin's eyes, and he rushed to continue. "Well, do you remember how my dad and I used to go the beach every Saturday?" Kaitlin nodded her head yes, urging him to continue. "When we used to go there, we would play on the beach and in the water and we would find all kinds of treasure out there. It was a lot of fun," Kyle said. Then he got a faraway look in his eyes and Kaitlin could tell that he was searching his memories. Kyle continued, "One day while we were at the beach, I noticed that there was this big rock wall stretching out over the last mile or so of the beach. I begged my dad to take me up there, but he would either ignore me and keep playing in the sand, or he would tell me that it was too dangerous to go up there."

Kyle paused, searching his thoughts again, and said, "When Dad couldn't go to the beach with me anymore I was so bummed. I moped around our yard for weeks, wishing that we could go back together and explore. Then one day it dawned on me that it was up to me to find out what was up there for myself. So that's what I did. I would go up there after I finished my homework and every chance that I could sneak away on the weekend."

"I always wondered what you were up to being gone so long," Kaitlin mused.

"Well," Kyle continued, "that's not the half of it. It turned out that there was a hole hidden down at the very far end of that rock wall. The hole was big enough for me to crouch down and crawl into. So I did what my dad would never do with me . . . I went inside and found out it was a cave."

"Weren't you scared?" Kaitlin asked.

"At first I was," Kyle said, "but then the more I looked around in that cave, the more curious I got. The first time I went I didn't have a flashlight with me, so it was very hard to see anything. I was forced to crawl through a narrow tunnel to get to the rest of the cave. Talk about creepy! I had no idea what was crawling around on the ground with me. I almost backed up and got out of that tunnel right then. But before I could make up my mind to go back, I noticed that the tunnel opened up into a much larger room. When I made it inside I found that I was able to stand up and walk around. It seemed that the farther I went into the cave, the darker it got. So I quit for the day and went back a few days later.

"The second time I brought a flashlight and was able to take a good look around. There really wasn't much to see in that first room. I was actually a little discouraged, but then I remembered that in my archaeology books there were pictures of caves that didn't have anything really interesting in them until you got farther in. I scanned the room with my flashlight and saw some stalagmites that had formed around the perimeter of the room. As I flashed my beam through the stalagmites I saw something protruding from between them. I really wasn't expecting to find anything there, so I almost missed a red object tucked between them. I had passed it up with the flashlight, but then I guess my brain registered that there was something I had missed. So I swept the beam back to that spot and saw that there was what appeared to be a piece of red material. It seemed odd to me at the time, and I still can't figure out how it got there, but it was there and that's all that matters. When I picked up the fabric I noticed that it was velvety and wrapped around something. When I unwrapped it, I found that tooth.

"Of course, finding that tooth made me extra curious. I just knew that there had to be more hidden treasures in that cave for me to find. I didn't go there very often at first because I didn't want

Mom getting upset or worried if I was gone too long or too often. Sometimes I would go after school, but only for an hour because I had to be back before she got home from work. The best times, though, were when I went on Saturdays. I had at least a few hours to explore the cave. Mom just thought I was hanging out at the beach, which, technically, I was. It was on those Saturdays that I was able to find more and more rooms to explore. I was pretty good about keeping track of the time and getting home before dinner. Well, that is until the other day. It was then that I found the key that you saw. I was so caught up in trying to figure out what that key was used for that I completely lost track of time. I'm still dumbfounded as to what a key could be used for in a cave, but I know that it was there for some reason.

"As far as those two men go, I have no idea who they are. I had never seen them before that day. When I went inside, one of them followed me in there and tried to talk with me. I didn't say a word or move so the man didn't know for certain that I was there. But then, when I ran out of the cave, the other, dark-haired man was crouching above the cave entrance, waiting for me to come out. I was already on my way down to the bike rack when the dark-haired man jumped down from above. Once I crossed the jagged part of the path, I took off running as fast as I could. There was no way he could keep up with me, thank goodness."

"Why would they be following *you*?" Kaitlin asked in disbelief.

"I really don't know," Kyle replied. "I've never seen them before. But I suspect that they were looking for something in that cave. They must have been watching me for some time. It seemed very strange that they just happened to be there the day that I found that key."

"Oh, how scary to think that they've been following you around like that!" Kaitlin said.

"Yeah, it is a little scary," Kyle admitted, "but I've decided to just be very careful. There must be something *very* valuable in there for them to be staking that cave out."

"I have so many questions," Kaitlin said, "but I think I need time to figure out what all of them are."

"That's OK," Kyle assured her. "I have to go home for now anyway. Would you like to meet me after school and take a trip to the cave?"

Kaitlin hesitated for a moment and looked a little panicked.

"Now who's the chicken?" Kyle teased.

"Oh, no way, Kyle! You can't compare me being a little worried because of two strange men sneaking around to you being afraid of a little mouse!" Kaitlin insisted.

"All right, you win," Kyle agreed. "But please, Kaitlin, come with me to the cave. I've wanted to show you the place for a long time."

Kaitlin thought to herself, *How can I refuse that?*

"OK, Kyle," she said. "I'll go with you."

"*GREAT!*" Kyle shouted excitedly. "I'll see you right after school. We'll meet here in your front yard and we'll go explore the cave."

"What if those men are there?" Kaitlin questioned.

"Don't worry, Kaitlin. I found another way out of the cave, so if they do show up we will just go out that way."

Kaitlin shrugged and headed toward her back door. "I guess I'll see you tomorrow then," she said.

"You bet!" Kyle said gleefully. "See you tomorrow. And Kaitlin, thanks for hiding the chest for me."

"No problem," she said with a forced smile. As she walked away, Kaitlin felt nothing short of trepidation at the thought of what they might encounter the next day.

CHAPTER 9

Kyle had a very hard time concentrating at school that Monday. In math class, working with numbers made him think about how many stalactites and stalagmites he could count in that cave. In science class, they were discussing fossils that are found in rocks, which of course made him think about what kinds of fossils he could possibly find in the rock walls of the cave. What he learned in the rest of his classes really had nothing at all to do with caves or anything that would remotely tie in with a cave. However, he still found himself drifting off into thoughts about what cool things he and Kaitlin might find that afternoon. More than once he was scolded by his teachers for not paying attention. One of the teachers even asked him if he wasn't feeling well. Kyle knew that his behavior today was foreign to his teachers. He usually paid very close attention to what he was learning in class. But today it seemed as if nothing else mattered except for the cave.

What made the cave seem all the more fascinating to him was the fact that those men had been hanging around. Kyle pondered his most recent discussion with Kaitlin and came to the conclusion that there had to be something very valuable hidden in there that those two wanted to get their hands on. As he pondered what it could possibly be, he finally came to the conclusion that it *must* have something to do with the key. He racked his brain trying to remember if there was anything that he had seen in the cave that the key would be used for.

At one point during the day he had let out a sigh of frustration because he couldn't think of a single thing that appeared to be anything more than a wall made of rock. He had been in his language arts class and was supposed to be taking a test. He recalled looking down at his test paper and realizing that he was only halfway through the questions. The worst part about it was that it had occurred to him that in five minutes class would be over. His teacher had walked over to his desk and glanced down at his test paper. She had bent over slightly and whispered to him "Kyle, did you study for your test?"

Kyle could still feel the heat of embarrassment that had crept into his cheeks. He had replied, "Yes, ma'am, I studied. I just seem to be having a hard time concentrating."

"Well," she had said, "I guess that even happens to me on occasion. Do your best to finish up before class is over. If you need to stay after class for a few minutes, I will write a tardy pass for your teacher next hour."

Kyle had exhaled a sigh of relief and said, "Thank you, ma'am. It won't happen again."

Kyle knew that if he had been one of those kids who messed around in class and who rarely turned in his homework on time, his teacher would not have been willing to do what she did. He had been very thankful that day for the lessons his mom and dad had instilled in him about being responsible and putting his whole heart into everything he did.

Although it had seemed that the day would stretch on forever, Kyle was finally nearing the end of it. His last period was gym class. Most days he didn't care for having his schedule set up this way. Most kids had time to grab a quick shower after their exercise was over with. But because this was the end of the day, Kyle had no choice but to quickly throw on his clothes, run to his locker to grab his books and backpack, and make it out to the bus just before it pulled away.

The reason it all seemed different today was that he needed a distraction. The rest of his classes forced him to think and reason things out, which only led to him getting lost in his thoughts about the cave. In PE they were playing basketball outside, which meant that he would be doing a lot of running up and down the court. The downside was that he would be extra stinky by the time class was over. The upside, however, was that he would be compelled to keep his attention focused on the ball. That would certainly help to keep his mind from continually returning to the cave.

By the time class was over, he rehashed the last forty-five minutes and smiled slightly to himself. For the most part his theory had been correct. He had only thought about the cave a few times. He quickly grabbed his jeans and T-shirt out of his locker and haphazardly threw them on. It didn't matter to him if he looked disheveled today.

The bell rang just as he was tying up his sneakers. "Oh, nuts!" Kyle exclaimed. "I can't be late for the bus today!" He took off in a full sprint toward his locker. Once he reached it he quickly dialed the combination, threw his books in his backpack, and slammed his locker door closed. Then he ran as if his life depended on it until he made it to the front door of the school.

He stepped outside and headed toward his bus. He was within ten feet of the big yellow beast when it started to pull away. *"NO! WAIT FOR ME!"* Kyle shouted amidst the deafening noise of the diesel engine. He flailed his arms about trying to get the bus driver's attention. Kyle watched as the bus drove a little farther down the school driveway. He anticipated that it would continue to move forward, but then it suddenly stopped. The doors burst open and Kyle quickly grabbed his backpack that he had dropped in the process of waving his arms around.

He sprinted toward the bus and bounded up the steps. Once he reached the top, he paused to thank the bus driver for stopping for him. "Don't thank me," he said. "Thank your buddy Allan. He's the one who saw you out there flapping your arms around like a crazy chicken!" he said with a chuckle.

Kyle stole a quick glance around the bus to find his friend. Allan was sitting way in the back of the bus, which was completely uncharacteristic for him. Kyle was glad that he had picked today to do something out of the ordinary. He walked to the rear of the bus and sat down next to Allan.

"Thanks, man!" Kyle said with sincere appreciation.

"Sure thing," Allan replied. "You looked so pathetic out there! I couldn't live with myself if I hadn't said anything. I have to admit, though, it was quite a funny sight!"

"I'm glad you got a good laugh out of it," Kyle said with a frown.

"Oh, relax, I'm the only one who saw you. At least I think so," Allan teased.

Allan squinted and inspected Kyle's face. "What happened to your forehead, pal?" he asked. "That's a heck of a goose egg!" he said with a hint of laughter.

Kaitlin, who was sitting with her friend Renee in the seat in front of them, turned around and faced the two boys. "It was my fault, Allan," she began. "Kyle was trying to help me get something out of my shed yesterday. When I went to open the door, I pulled too hard and it accidentally smacked him on the forehead."

Kyle shot a look at Kaitlin that could only be interpreted as *"WHY DID YOU SAY THAT?"*

Allan got a big cheesy grin on his face and turned his attention to Kyle. "Wow, Kyle," he teased, "since when do you let a little girl beat you up?"

Kyle started to defend himself, "I didn't le . . ." but he was unable to finish before Kaitlin cut in with, "I didn't beat him up, Allan. But if you don't cut it out, I *will* beat *you* up!"

"Yeah!" her friend Renee agreed. "And I'll help her!"

"Oh no!" Allan said with mock horror. "I'm quaking in my boots!"

Kyle, who hadn't been able to utter a complete sentence without an interruption, was finally able to speak. "All right, you guys . . . and girls. That's enough. Allan, it was an accident and nothing else. Nobody else hears about your theory or I'll tell everyone what happens when you sleep!"

Allan's face turned a shade of white that could have rivaled the teachers' marker board. "You wouldn't!" he seethed.

"Oh, sure I would," Kyle countered, "if you insist on spreading this nonsense about a girl beating me up!"

Allan scrunched his eyebrows and thought for a minute before replying, "Fine, you have my word. I won't say anything about you being beat up by a girl."

"Glad to hear that," Kyle said.

"Hey, Kyle," Renee asked with a teasing grin at Allan, "what exactly *does* Allan do when he's sleeping?"

"I can't tell you that! I promised!" Kyle said, feigning surprise. But when Allan turned his head to look out the window, Kyle pinched his nose with one hand and used his other hand to wave back and forth in front of his face. His eyes rolled back in his head as if he were about to pass out.

"*Ohhh!*" Renee said with a smile, and Kaitlin started to giggle.

"Hey," Allan said vehemently, "you promised you wouldn't say anything!"

"I didn't *say* anything, did I, girls?" Kyle asked with a wink in their direction.

"Nope," Renee answered, "he didn't say a word."

Allan gave Kyle a look and said, "Sure . . ." He remained quiet the rest of the trip to his stop.

When Allan stood up to leave, Kyle grabbed his arm and said, "It's all in fun, right, Allan?"

Allan stopped for a second and looked at Kyle. "I suppose," he said.

"OK, then, see you tomorrow," Kyle said. "Thanks for stopping the bus for me."

"Yep," Allan replied, and with that he walked down the bus aisle and down the steps.

As soon as the bus started moving again, Kaitlin turned around in her seat to look at Kyle. "So, what's the plan for this afternoon?" she asked.

Kyle sat there in stunned silence for a minute. He looked at Kaitlin but didn't answer her right away. All he could think of was, *Why would she try to talk about this when everyone is listening? At the very least, I know Renee heard her. She may start asking questions.* Luckily it didn't seem as if Renee thought anything out of the ordinary was going on. As a matter of fact, she seemed to have drifted off into her own little world as she looked out the bus window. Her stop would be next, so Kaitlin wouldn't have to wait long for the two of them to make their plans.

In the meantime, he had to come up with some kind of reply to Kaitlin's question. "Well, the first thing I have to do is go home and take a shower . . ." he answered, but before he could make any further comments about having to do homework and helping his mom get ready for dinner, Kaitlin quipped, "Is that what smells so bad? I thought the bus had hit a skunk!"

Obviously, Renee had been at least half-listening to their conversation, because she burst out laughing at Kaitlin's comment. Then she joined in on the fun, saying, "Boy, Kyle, it really is too bad for you that you have gym at the very end of the day! And it's even worse for the rest of us on the bus! Thank goodness these windows open or we'd all be passed out!"

Kyle wasn't thrilled about the direction the conversation had gone, but at least he didn't have to worry about talking about going to the cave in front of Renee. That was the last thing he wanted. If more people learned about the cave, then he would never be able to figure out what that key was used for. "Hardy, har, har!" he responded to Kaitlin and Renee.

He noticed the bus was slowing to a stop, and the bus driver called out, "Here you go, Renee."

Renee and Kaitlin both stood up. Kaitlin moved out into the aisle to let Renee move past her. "Bye, Renee," Kaitlin said with a little wave at her friend.

"See you tomorrow," Renee answered with a wave and a smile, and she made her way to the front of the bus.

Once her friend was safely down the steps, Kaitlin plopped down into the seat next to Kyle. "What was that all about?" she asked.

"Are you kidding me?" Kyle almost shrieked in disbelief. "You know very well that if Renee were to hear us talking about the cave, eventually the whole school would find out! I think she's nice and all, but, boy, oh boy, does that girl have a motor mouth!"

Kyle saw a look cross Kaitlin's face and he realized that Kaitlin had taken offense on behalf of her friend. She almost started chastising Kyle for his rude comment, but then thought better of it. *Actually,* she had to admit to herself, *Kyle is right. She would blab to the whole school.* She was not about to admit that to Kyle though. Instead, she said to him, "Oh, come on! She's not that bad."

Kyle had to bite his lip to keep from saying anything more. He knew that even if Kaitlin didn't admit it, deep down she knew that what he had said was the truth. "Well, whether it's Renee or anyone else on this bus, I don't want *anyone* to hear about this!" he insisted. "If even one of these kids finds out about that cave, it will be crawling with people. And if that happens I'll never be able to find out what that key is for. Those two men will disappear out of town as fast as they showed up."

Kaitlin looked at Kyle as if she were about to say she would like it if that happened. Kyle read her expression and said, "I know you wouldn't mind it a bit if they *did* leave, but they just can't! I can't really explain why I feel this way, but I have a feeling that somehow they are going to help me find out what that key is for."

"Kyle Marshall, what are you talking about? Have you lost your marbles completely?" Kaitlin asked. "You do remember that the dark-haired man clobbered you in the forehead as he was trying to escape with your treasure . . . right?"

"Kaitlin," he replied quietly, "I do remember that very well. I have a bump on my head the size of Texas that won't let me forget! But there was something about that older man . . . I'm not sure exactly how to explain this . . . That day when I first saw them my first instinct was to run for my life. But there was something about the older man that made me think that he was harmless. He almost looked disappointed that I would not come out to talk to him. I'm not very fond of the dark-haired guy. He's the one that worries me. Especially after the stunt he pulled yesterday. But still, I don't think he set out to *hurt* me. I just think he was trying to find my key and tooth and we just startled him. Well, at least Chester startled him. I just happened to be in his path when he tried to make his getaway."

Kaitlin still didn't appear to be convinced, but she shrugged her shoulders. Obviously, Kyle sensed something about the older man that had convinced him he would be able to help him. Kyle, she had to admit, was pretty good at surmising the character of a person, even if he didn't really *know* them.

"All right, Kyle, I'll play this your way. But so help me, if something bad happens to us . . ."

"It won't, Kaitlin," he assured her. "Who does that older man remind you of?" he asked.

Kaitlin stared off into space and then she answered, "It seems like I've seen him on TV before. No, wait, not really on a show; I think it may have been on a commercial." Kaitlin paused again briefly, but then she jumped up out of the seat and exclaimed, "I remember! He looks just like the man who owns that chicken restaurant. You know, the one with the recipe with the secret herbs and spices? I think his name was . . . oh, drat! What *is* his name? Colonel . . . Kentucky . . . yeah, that's it!"

Kyle noticed that Kaitlin looked very pleased with herself for figuring out the puzzle. He smiled a bit and said, "Yep. That's the one! But I don't think it's the same man. I mean, what would he care about a stupid old cave anyway?"

Kaitlin nodded in agreement and said, "I don't think it's the same man either, but it sure is funny how much the two of them look alike!"

"Well, anyway," Kyle said, "I still don't think we have anything to worry about with those two. Not really. I'm hoping they will just keep their distance and let us do our exploring. I just can't shake this feeling that somehow 'Mr. Kentucky' knows something that will help us."

"I guess we'll see," Kaitlin said, just as the bus was pulling up to their stop.

"I guess," Kyle replied. As they walked off the final step and onto the grass below, Kyle told Kaitlin, "I really *do* need to go take a shower. But I won't be long."

"Yeah, you better do that, Kyle, because I don't think I could handle being trapped in that cave with you and your terrible BO!" Kaitlin said with a wink.

"Oh, whatever!" Kyle exclaimed, and he started to walk up the sidewalk to his front door. He turned around as Kaitlin was heading to her house and shouted out, "Give me about fifteen minutes and I'll meet you out here. I'll shower really fast, but then I'll have to grab a few things from the garage for our little expedition."

"OK. Kyle . . ." Kaitlin sounded as if she were going to add something else, but then she changed her mind. "Never mind. I'll see you out here in fifteen minutes." Then she turned and disappeared in through her front door. Kyle was left standing there thinking, *Girls! I don't think I'll EVER have them figured out!*

CHAPTER 10

K yle had showered and changed and was now in the garage searching for things he and Kaitlin would need to bring with them to the cave. In one hand, he held an old beat-up backpack that he had used for school two years ago. With his other hand, he grabbed two medium-sized flashlights and put them in the pack. His dad had a larger flashlight that was much more powerful and would certainly shed more light in the dark cave, but Kyle had learned that the large flashlight was much too cumbersome to hold for any length of time. Back when he had first started his cave explorations, he had thought about asking for a headlamp for his birthday. Kyle sighed as he thought of how great it would be to not have to hold a flashlight the entire time. However, he had realized that if he did ask for that as a gift, more than likely it would raise some questions from his parents. So, as quickly as the thought had come to him, he had dismissed it.

He shook himself out of the memory and forced himself to focus on the task at hand. "Come on, Kyle," he chided himself, "get it together. We don't have that long to be at the cave, so don't waste the time wishing for something you can't have." He attempted to clear his mind and thought, *OK, what else do I need to bring with?* It occurred to him that on occasion he had gotten some bruises and scrapes from crawling around in the cave, so he ran back into the house and grabbed a few Band-Aids and some gauze out of the bathroom. He decided it might be better not to let Kaitlin know he had them. It wasn't that he wanted to keep anything from her, but he was almost certain that if she saw them it would send her into panic mode and she would not want to even try to go in the cave.

He went back out into the garage and started rummaging through his dad's cabinet to see if anything in there might be useful. There he found a few mason jars with nails and screws in them. It seemed that the jars would be ideal to use if they found something in the cave that was worth saving. Kyle thought about crawling through the narrow tunnels and what might happen if his backpack were to accidentally hit the ceiling of the tunnel; or worse yet, if he tripped and fell and landed on the pack. If one jar broke, Kyle reasoned, that would be enough of a mess to clean up. Two broken jars would be a disaster. So he emptied the jar with the nails and placed that inside the pack. He saw some plastic zipper bags that could also come in handy for temporarily storing whatever they might find. He grabbed a handful of bags of various sizes and stuffed those in and around the jar to give it a bit more protection.

Next, he found a tool that his dad called "the gripper," which was collapsible and would come in handy if they needed to reach an object that was caught in a tight space. He found a roll of paper towels, thinking, *Just in case we find something that is breakable that we need to wrap up.* Looking at the paper towels, he thought that it might be a good idea to place those between the jar and the part of the backpack that would face the ceiling in the tunnel. *After all,* he pondered, *a little extra cushion can't hurt.*

Kyle took a look around the garage and felt fairly satisfied that he had found everything they could need for today's expedition. He began to head out the side door of the garage when he realized that he had forgotten to grab some water to drink. On his earliest visits, he had not had the presence of mind to bring any with him. Once he was there he had been much too excited to care. After some time had gone by, though, he had felt parched and wished he had a bottle of water.

The cave itself was damp, and he had found that there were pools of water spread randomly throughout the cave. But the thought of drinking that water had made a shiver run down his spine. *I'm not a scaredy cat,* Kyle had thought to himself, *but it's hard telling what is in that water.* He had imagined all kinds of little amoebas swimming around in it and the algae that he had seen on the surface of the pools. Those two things alone were enough to make him not want to drink it. *Besides,* he had thought and then cringed, *you never know what kind of animals have used that water to bathe in . . . or worse!* He was certain that if *he* felt that way, then there was no way that Kaitlin would want to drink it. With that settled in his mind, he went back into the kitchen and grabbed three bottles of water.

Kyle had never been a Boy Scout, but he liked to live by their motto to "always be prepared." On numerous occasions, he had found himself to be exactly the opposite of prepared. The trouble that had ensued had caused him to vow to himself that he would "never do that again!" He gave one last glance around, just to make sure he was not going to forget something important. He couldn't see anything that jumped out at him, so he said to himself, "OK, now we should be ready to go."

Kyle slung the backpack over his shoulders and propped open the door on the side of the garage. He walked over to his bike, flipped the kickstand up with his foot, and proceeded to wheel it out the door. He parked the bike and closed and locked the door behind him. He then grabbed the handles and swung his right leg over the frame of the bike until he was straddling it. With his feet, he slowly walked his bike around the side of the garage and through his yard. His eyes were trained on the ground, scanning for every little rut that might cause him and his bike to take a tumble. He continued to move forward toward Kaitlin's driveway without ever bothering to look up.

"Hey!" he heard Kaitlin yell. "Watch where you're going!"

At the same moment that Kaitlin had uttered "Hey," Kyle had been startled, and out of reflex, he gripped the brakes so hard that the bike was upended and he was launched off his bike seat and into the yard.

"Argh!" Kyle growled, rubbing his throbbing knee. "What did you do that for?"

"*Me?*" Kaitlin replied in astonishment. "All I did was try to get you to pay attention! You almost ran right into me!"

Kyle looked at Kaitlin and saw the puzzled and hurt look on her face. *Oh great,* he thought, *I blew it again!* Kaitlin looked at him expectantly, and Kyle could tell she was waiting for an apology. He was still a tad irritated, but he realized that the irritation was because of the pain in his knee and not because Kaitlin had done anything wrong. He slowly stood up, picked up his bike, and then turned to face Kaitlin. "You're right, Kaitlin. I'm sorry," he said with all sincerity. "I was just so excited that I forgot to look where I was going."

"Boy," Kaitlin teased, "I bet telling me you're sorry was about as much fun as having a tooth pulled."

Kyle, who was thoroughly offended by her comment, defended his honor by saying, "That's not true . . . I meant it." Then he noticed the wide grin on her face and he laughed. "OK," he admitted, "it's not the easiest thing in the world to say . . . but I really did mean it."

"I know that," Kaitlin reassured him, and she patted him on his arm.

"Well, now that that's over with, can we get moving?" Kyle asked. "We'll only have about an hour to look around by the time we get there and I'm hoping that you'll see enough that it will make you want to go back another time."

"Kyle Marshall, you're lucky you're getting me to go this time!" Kaitlin insisted. "I'm not going to promise there will be a *next* time."

Kyle noticed a look on Kaitlin's face that told him she was feeling concerned about their trip to the cave. "Kaitlin, please don't worry! I promise that I won't let anything bad happen to you," he assured her.

"Look, Kyle," Kaitlin interjected. "It's not you or the cave that I'm really worried about. It's those men. I know you say you feel like they aren't out to hurt you . . ." She paused briefly and then sighed and began again. "But what if you're wrong?"

"I guess you're right," Kyle admitted. "I really can't be sure that they won't try to hurt us. But I am sure that you are my best friend and I would never let them lay a finger on you."

Kaitlin didn't say anything for a few seconds, but then relented and said, "All right, then. Let's go."

Kyle sensed that she was still feeling uneasy about the situation, but he had to admit that she was showing a bravery he rarely saw in her. "Thanks, Kaitlin," he said. He wasn't sure if his words were enough to help Kaitlin understand how important this was to him . . . and how much it meant to him that she was willing to go in spite of her fear. But he determined that he was going to prove to her that not only would he protect her, but that once she saw the cave for herself, she would be just as excited as he was.

The two of them set off on their bikes, riding side by side as they traveled the streets of their neighborhood. A slight breeze was coming in off the ocean, and Kyle noticed that Kaitlin was struggling to keep her hair from blowing into her face.

"Are you OK?" Kyle asked. "Do you need to pull over?"

"Maybe just for a few seconds," Kaitlin replied gratefully.

The two veered off to the shoulder of the road. When Kaitlin came to a stop, Kyle watched as she reached into her jeans pocket and pulled out a hair tie. She quickly swiped a handful of her hair off of her neck, and within seconds, she had the hair tie securely in place.

"Thanks, Kyle," she said. "I guess it will be better to have my hair out of my face while we're in the cave anyway," she said with a slight smile.

"Probably," Kyle agreed. "All right, if you're ready, just make sure that when we get out to the highway that you follow me. I know you know where the beach is, but there's a certain path that we'll have to take to get to the cave."

"Sure thing, Mr. Bossy," Kaitlin said, indignantly. "I'm pretty sure that I could find it on my own, but have it your way."

Kyle shook his head, not quite understanding what had just happened. "Kaitlin, I…" he began, then paused to rethink what he was about to say. He then finished with, "I just thought it might make it easier since I've been there before."

Kaitlin hesitated briefly and then replied, "Fine. But next time *I* get to lead the way."

It was not lost on Kyle that Kaitlin had spoken the words "next time" and he felt slightly encouraged.

There was no conversation for the rest of the trip as they made their way to the cave. Kyle gestured occasionally to let Kaitlin know where they would be making a turn and looked back frequently to make sure she was right behind him. As they neared the beach, Kyle came to a stop and Kaitlin did the same.

"The sand is very hard to ride a bike on, Kaitlin," he said, "so it will be better if we leave our bikes here for now. We can lock them up at that bike rack over there and then we will walk the rest of the way."

Kaitlin nodded and pulled up to the rack. As she parked and locked her bike she had to admit that she was secretly relieved they wouldn't be trekking through the sand on the bikes. *I know what a klutz I am,* Kaitlin thought to herself, *and that would be an accident waiting to happen.*

Once the bikes were secured, Kyle explained to Kaitlin about the path they would take to the cave. "We'll follow that path that you see running right alongside of the cliff most of the way," he said. "Once we get to a certain point, we're going to have to do some climbing. You'll have to be very careful because the part that we have to climb has some loose rocks. But don't worry, I'll point them out to you."

Kaitlin groaned. *Great!* she thought. *Not only do we have to worry about those men, but now I have to somehow avoid tumbling off the cliff!* Kyle, who was reveling in his thoughts about finally being able to show Kaitlin the cave, took no notice of her dissatisfaction.

He proceeded to walk through the sand, completely oblivious to the fact that every few seconds Kaitlin was turning her head this way and that way, searching for any sign of the two men. The beach was not at all crowded that day due to the sky being overcast, and that was fine by Kaitlin. *That way,* she thought, *if those guys are lurking around they will be much easier to spot.* She felt herself relax a little as, the closer they got to the cave, she realized that she had not seen anything to give her concern.

The two reached what appeared to be the end of the path at the very far end of the cliff wall.

"Kyle? I don't see the cave," Kaitlin said. "I've been looking up at the wall to find the entrance and all it looks like is a bunch of rocks. There aren't any holes in them."

"Correct!" Kyle shouted gleefully. "That's because there aren't any holes in there," he said with a knowing smile.

"Kyle Marshall, if there isn't a cave out here, then why on earth did you drag me out here?" she demanded.

"Silly girl," Kyle responded. "I never said there wasn't an entrance. I only said that you can't see the entrance from where we are." Kyle's grin was so big it spread across his whole face.

Kaitlin, who was not smiling at all, slugged his arm and asked, "OK, then, where *is* it?"

Kyle pointed to the very end of the cliff and answered, "Well, we climb straight up from here. When we get about halfway up the wall, we will reach the path. Once we are on it, the path will curve around the end there. Most people don't ever bother to look any further than where we are now because they just assume that this is the end of the wall and there is nothing else to see. But they're wrong. The entrance to the cave is tucked into the rocks in the side of the cliffs."

"Oh," Kaitlin said with a look of bewilderment. "You know, I've lived here my whole life and never realized that there was any more to that cliff than you could see from the beach. I guess I never took the time to look any further than here. That's pretty cool, Kyle!"

"It sure is!" Kyle agreed enthusiastically. "I'm ready to get going. Are you?"

Kaitlin looked up the face of the cliff, sighed, then shrugged her shoulders. "I guess so," she answered, sounding a little unsure. "I've come this far. I might as well find the pot at the end of the rainbow."

"We just might!" Kyle exclaimed, beaming brighter than the sun. "OK, here we go. Just follow me."

Kaitlin grumbled under her breath and mimicked, "Just follow me." Having gotten that out of her system, she said, "Sure thing, Kyle."

Kyle reached one hand up and grabbed a rock above him. He placed his foot on a rock that was up a little higher than the level of the path and pushed himself up. Next, he did the same thing with his other hand and his other foot, only this time choosing rocks that were a bit higher than the first. Kaitlin watched as he repeated the process, and before long she felt that she had the hang of it. She began to climb as Kyle had done, and before long she had caught up to him and was side by side with him.

As she was hanging there, gripping the rocks for dear life, she shrieked out at Kyle, "Why did you stop? I'm going to lose my momentum!"

She watched as Kyle pointed to a rock that was slightly above her and to her right. "Do you see that rock?" he asked. Kaitlin nodded. "Good!" Kyle said. "Stay away from it. That's one of the loose rocks. The best thing to do now is to grab a rock that's above you and to the left."

"I don't think I can do that, Kyle!" Kaitlin whined. "I've been starting out on my right side because it's easier for me."

Kyle, who was still clinging to the rock wall himself, said vehemently, "I understand, Kaitlin. But remember I told you that there were going to be loose rocks? I also said that I would point them out to you so you wouldn't fall. That's what I'm doing. I don't want you to fall, Kaitlin. I know you can do this, even if you don't think you can. Besides, we're almost up to the path."

Kaitlin said nothing, but after a brief pause, Kyle saw that she was swinging her left hand up to catch the rock above her. He could tell that she was straining, and he knew it was because her left side was weaker than her right. *Come on, Kaitlin. I know you can do it,* Kyle said silently to himself, rooting for her. He watched as she brought her left foot up to the rock above it. Before he knew it, she was back in her climbing groove and had reached the path that led to the cave. Kyle smiled to himself but did not want to let her see it. He watched as she brushed her hands off on her jeans and then plopped down in a heap on the path.

Kyle finished his climb and once he reached the top, he sat down next to Kaitlin. "Good job!" he encouraged her. "I knew you could do it! We'll rest for a minute, but don't forget that time is short today."

"I know, I know!" Kaitlin said. "I'm ready, I guess. I just wanted to give my legs and arms a break. They feel like Jell-O!"

"Yeah," Kyle said, "mine felt like that too the first few times I climbed this wall."

The two friends stood up and then continued down the path until it led them around the side of the wall. Kaitlin took a good look down the path and realized that Kyle had indeed been right. She marveled at how much she had missed out on, and she marveled even more at Kyle for being brave enough to come exploring up here by himself. She smiled at him and told herself, *Well, if he can do it, I certainly can too.*

Once they rounded the corner, they finally reached the entrance to the cave. Kaitlin realized that she would have missed it if she were up here by herself. The hole that Kyle had talked about seemed barely distinguishable among the rocks. But indeed, it was there. She watched as Kyle got down on his hands and knees and faced the entrance. Kaitlin followed his lead and got in line behind him.

Kyle turned around with the biggest smile she had ever seen on his face. "Good to go?" he asked.

"Um. Yeah," she replied, "but hang on just one second." She turned her head from side to side, scanning the area just to be certain they weren't being watched. When she felt that she was satisfied that no one was in sight, she turned to Kyle and said, "All right. I'm ready now."

Kyle eagerly led the way into the cave tunnel. As Kaitlin followed closely behind him, she noticed that it was pitch-black. The only light was the remnant of that from the outside. The farther they moved along, the darker it got. And the darker it got, the more nervous Kaitlin grew.

"Kyle, is your flashlight not working?" she asked with a hint of hysteria creeping into her voice.

"It works fine, but it's too hard to hold right now while I'm on all fours," he responded. "As soon as we get to the first room I'll turn it on."

Kaitlin was not thrilled about his answer, but she continued on behind him, staying as close to him as she possibly could. With every "step" they made forward, the cave grew darker and she felt as if the walls were closing in on her. Kaitlin heard a noise and she went scurrying forward, propelling herself straight into Kyle's back end.

"OOF!" she heard him say. "Kaitlin, what's going on? What did you do that for?"

Kaitlin's breathing was heavy, and it took her a minute before she responded. "Kyle, did you *say* something?"

"You mean just now, when you bumped into me?" Kyle asked, surprised.

"No!" Kaitlin said emphatically. "I mean just before that. Please tell me that it was you that I heard!"

"Um, I'm sorry, Kaitlin, but it wasn't me."

Kaitlin held very still for what seemed like an eternity. When she was finally able to speak, she said in a whisper that Kyle could barely hear, "If it wasn't you, then someone else is outside of this cave!"

CHAPTER 11

"**K**aitlin," Kyle said, "I didn't hear a thing! It may have been the wind that you thought you heard but trust me when I say that there is no one out there!"

"NO . . ." Kaitlin shouted hysterically, but then, realizing that whoever was out there would hear her, she lowered her voice and whispered, "Don't you dare talk to me like I'm imagining things, Kyle! I know the difference between men's voices and the wind! I'm telling you that there is no doubt that those two men are out there."

"OK, Kaitlin, let's assume that you *did* hear someone talking outside. You can't be sure that it was them, you know," Kyle said, trying to calm Kaitlin.

"Oh really?" Kaitlin hissed. "Then you tell me, oh wise one, who else would be up here near the mouth of the cave that no one else in town even knows exists?"

Kyle pondered her words. He had to admit that she had a good point. "You may be right," Kyle began, and then Kaitlin interrupted sharply with "*MAY BE?*"

"Well," Kyle said, measuring his next words, "you are probably right. I guess the chances of it being anyone else are pretty slim."

"Exactly!" Kaitlin agreed, and then she finished with, "So what do we do now? How are we going to get away from them?"

Kyle could feel all the energy and enthusiasm he had felt earlier drain away in a matter of seconds. He realized that what she was saying meant that her only thought was of getting out of the cave safely and avoiding those men at all costs. That also meant that there would be zero cave exploration today. Kyle could feel his frustration rising, and if he wasn't very careful, he could end up directing that frustration at Kaitlin. However, he realized it was not her fault that things had ended up this way. He was the one who had assured her that there was nothing to worry about, and yet, apparently, what she feared the most was right outside of the cave.

"I still haven't heard anyone talking, Kaitlin. Are you absolutely sure that you heard them?" Kyle asked, almost pleading with her to be wrong.

"Well, if you would just be quiet for a minute and listen," Kaitlin answered, "you *will* be able to hear them."

Kyle took her advice. He didn't say a word and he didn't even move a muscle. The silence and the darkness that surrounded them seemed as if it could swallow them whole. Kyle was becoming more agitated by the second, struggling to hear any hint of words being spoken outside of the cave. After about half a minute had gone by with no sound, he opened his mouth to say, "See, there is no one out there." But just as soon as his lips parted to say the words, he heard them. He couldn't tell exactly what they were saying, but he *could* tell that there were two people out there talking.

"See?" Kaitlin whined. "I TOLD YOU THEY WERE OUT THERE!"

He truly did not want her to be right, but she was. Kyle sat there feeling defeated, but then his ears perked up when he faintly heard the words, "I saw them go in there. We need to follow them."

"How is that possible?" Kyle seethed. "We didn't see any sign of them the whole way to the cave!"

"I don't know, Kyle," Kaitlin answered. "I didn't see them, and I looked everywhere for them. It doesn't make any sense to me either. But I do know that we need to get out of here! I heard one of them say that they should follow us in here!"

"I know," Kyle replied, "I heard it too." He paused again and then finally said, "OK, I guess our only choice is to get out of the cave by the back door. Come on, Kaitlin. Follow me."

Kyle began to crawl forward, and Kaitlin followed closely behind him. "Are you going to turn on the flashlight, Kyle?" she asked.

"Are you crazy?" Kyle asked. "You do realize that if I turn the light on then they will for sure know where we are, right?"

Kaitlin hadn't thought about that because she was in too big of a hurry to get out of the cave. "Yeah, I guess you're right," she admitted. "Are you sure you know the way to the back door without having the light on?"

"Kaitlin," Kyle said, "I may have been wrong about those guys following us, but I do know how to get us out of here. If I didn't have an escape route, I never would have brought you up here."

"OK, then," Kaitlin said with urgency, "get us *out of here!*"

Once again, Kyle began crawling forward and soon had reached the entrance to the first room. Kaitlin noticed that he was now standing up, so she attempted to do the same. Apparently, she had not quite made it out of the tunnel, though, because she felt the top of her head collide with the tunnel's rocky ceiling.

"OW!" Kaitlin shrieked, hopping around while rubbing her head.

"Kaitlin, SHH!" Kyle reminded her.

Kaitlin had tears running down her cheeks, because the blow to her head had been a pretty significant one. "I can't help it!" she whimpered. "It hurts!"

"I know, and I'm sorry," Kyle said. "I was going to tell you when to stand up, but you must have been really anxious." He rubbed her head and felt a large knot. He didn't want to alarm her, so he said, "As soon as we get home, we'll put some ice on your head. That will make it feel much better."

"Boy, aren't we a pair!" Kaitlin said in a voice that almost sounded as if she were laughing. "First you get whacked on the forehead, twice, and now I get this beauty on the top of my head! His and hers goose eggs!"

Well, Kyle thought, *she can't be too hurt. She still has her sense of humor.* He reached out to Kaitlin to make sure she was steady enough to walk.

"I'm OK, Kyle," she said. "Just lead the way out of here."

Kyle shook his head and walked straight down the middle of the room. Kaitlin's eyes were slowly adjusting to the dark and she noticed that at the end of the room there were two entrances that led to either another room or a tunnel. At this point, she was hoping it was a room. She had had enough of tunnels for a while. Kyle motioned for her to follow him through the entrance on the left. She did as he did and was relieved to find out that it did indeed lead to another room. This room seemed much smaller than the first, so they were only in it for about a minute before they approached yet another set of entrances.

Once again, Kaitlin saw Kyle motion for her to enter the tunnel to the left. This opened into a much larger room, probably about five times the size of the first one they had stepped into. She couldn't be sure, but she thought that off to her right she saw a variety of openings in the rock wall. Kaitlin had a feeling that if they had been able to do their exploring today, they would have ended up going into one of those entrances. But now their mission was only to escape, so Kyle veered to the left and through another opening.

They both paused when they heard some noises coming from behind them. Kyle heard the grunt of a man's voice, as if he was having a difficult time navigating the rough terrain. *That has to be Colonel Kentucky,* he thought. "Kaitlin, we better get moving!" he insisted.

"I know," Kaitlin replied hoarsely, "I heard them. Do you think they're going to catch up to us?"

Kyle surveyed the room around him and said, "No, I don't think so, Kaitlin. They are still pretty far behind us. By the time they reach this spot, and that's if they even figured out which way we went, we will long since be out of here. All we have to do now is crawl through this tunnel that's straight ahead and we will be home free."

"Another tunnel?" Kaitlin asked with exasperation in her voice. "I didn't realize we would have to do that again!"

"Well, do you want to get out," Kyle asked, "or do you want to turn around and come face to face with those two?"

"OK, you're right," she replied. "I just don't like the feeling of being caught in a tight space. Especially when I can't see. I guess I'm kind of, what's that word . . . ?"

"Claustrophobic," Kyle answered for her.

"Yeah, that's it," Kaitlin agreed.

"Well, don't worry, we'll be out of here in a jiff," Kyle said.

Kaitlin took a deep breath, squared her shoulders, and said, "OK, I'm as ready as I'm going to be. Let's do this!"

Kyle said nothing in reply but took a few more steps and then proceeded to get on his hands and feet like he had done when they first entered the cave. He began to creep forward, ever so slowly and carefully. Kaitlin thought he seemed a little hesitant, as if he wasn't quite sure of where he was going.

Well, she reasoned, *at least he knows more about where he is going than I do.* She followed him along, literally right on his feet, as they made their way through the tunnel. "Are we there yet, Kyle?" she asked.

"Almost," he replied.

Just then, they heard the sound of two men talking off in the distance. Kaitlin was feeling rather worried, but just as she felt an attack of panic coming on, she saw a hint of light ahead.

"See, I told you!" Kyle exulted. "We're home free."

"Home," Kaitlin repeated. "That word has never sounded so good!"

A few more "steps" and they were crawling out into the salt-soaked air and back onto the path. Kaitlin took a moment to look around and noticed that this part of the path did not look familiar. She realized that it could just be disorientation setting in after being in the cave, but she asked Kyle, "Where are we, exactly?"

"Well, do you remember once we got to the entrance of the cave that the path went down more towards the highway?" Kyle asked.

Kaitlin pictured the path and nodded.

Kyle, seeing that she was picturing it in her mind, continued, "That path continues around what would be considered the back side of the beach. That's where we are now. The path slopes down from here and then winds around back to the parking lot at the beach. We will have a much easier time getting down than we had coming up."

"Well, that's a relief!" Kaitlin sighed. For the first time since they had entered the cave, she felt herself begin to relax.

She and Kyle made their way down the path until they were right back at the bicycle rack. Kaitlin quickly undid her lock and prepared to hop on her bike so they could make their way home. She looked at Kyle and noticed that he didn't seem to be in quite as big of a hurry as she was.

"Come on, Kyle," she insisted, "we have to get out of here! They'll be right behind us."

Kyle just stared back up at the path and then slowly shook his head as if he were shaking himself out of a trance. "I know," he replied reluctantly. "I just didn't expect things to go this way."

"I'm sorry, Kyle," Kaitlin said, without sounding very sorry at all.

Kyle finally unlocked his bike, swung his leg over, and sat on the seat. He looked intently toward the cave one more time and then he said, "All right, let's go."

The two of them were silent for the majority of the trip home. When they finally reached their neighborhood, Kyle asked Kaitlin, "What are the chances that you'll want to go back there with me tomorrow?"

"HA!" Kaitlin said, in a voice that let Kyle know that she did not like the suggestion. "After what we just went through, do you really think I would want to go back there again? For that matter, why would you want to go back there again? It's obvious that those two are watching every move you make. So every time you go there they will be there too."

"So, is that a no?" Kyle asked, giving her a silly, pleading little smile.

"Yes, that's a no!" Kaitlin said emphatically. "The only way that you would get me back in that cave is if you tied me up and dragged me in there!"

Just then they each pulled into their own driveway. Kaitlin looked at Kyle and saw that he had a very sad look on his face. She felt sincerely sorry that he was disappointed, but she was determined never to go back to that cave again.

"Kyle, I'm sorry, but I can't take that chance again. That was way too close. And I wish you wouldn't either," she said in her best motherly voice.

Kyle, who was not so easily dissuaded, said, "You might be afraid of them, but I'm not. The only reason why I left today is because I knew how scared you were. Well, fine, if you won't go with me, I'll go by myself. I've done it so many times before that it's no big deal."

"Kyle, are you sure you want to do that?" Kaitlin questioned.

"You bet I do!" Kyle insisted. "I'm not going to be on the bus tomorrow, Kaitlin. I'm going to ride my bike to school and then go to the cave right after school lets out."

"I think you're nuts," she said, "but OK. Kyle, please be careful. I don't want them to hurt you."

"I'll be fine," Kyle said gruffly, and then he headed to his front door, went inside, and slammed the door behind him.

CHAPTER 12

T he next day, Kyle did as he had told Kaitlin and rode his bike to school. That morning, as he was pulling out of his driveway, he saw Kaitlin getting on the bus with the other kids. He gave a quick glance her way and noticed that she had a sad look on her face. If he was truthful with himself, he *did* understand why Kaitlin was worried about going back into the cave. He really couldn't blame her for being scared of the two men. After all, he really didn't know anything about them either. However, for some reason that he could not explain, he still felt as if he would not be harmed by them. As a result, he was more determined than ever to go back to the cave after school.

He proceeded to school with a million thoughts racing around in his head. When he pulled up to the bike rack, he reminded himself that he was going to have to focus on his studies that day. But, as the day went on, he noticed that it was nearly impossible to follow through with his intentions. The image of Kaitlin's sad facial expression this morning kept popping into his mind. He also struggled with the frustration of not being able to show her anything in the cave. His thoughts continuously drifted off to what could have been yesterday. He could imagine the two of them exploring rooms of the cave that he had not yet gotten to himself. He pictured them coming upon some amazing new find that he could add to his collection.

In his language arts class later that day, his teacher noticed that he seemed distracted. The class was working on an assignment that she had handed out for them to complete in class, and she noticed that Kyle really wasn't doing any writing. In fact, she noticed that he seemed to be staring off into space. She approached his desk and asked him to step outside in the hallway with her. When she had closed the door behind them, she asked, "Kyle, is everything OK with you? I'm having a hard time understanding why you've been so distracted the last couple of days."

Kyle realized that he couldn't tell her exactly why he was so out of it, but he could at least give her a partial explanation. "Well, ma'am, I've been feeling a little down today. Kaitlin and I sort of got into a fight yesterday afternoon and we haven't really spoken since. I guess it's just been on my mind all day."

His teacher nodded and said, "I can understand that, Kyle. We all have things that seem to be left unsettled that cause us to lose our focus. I hope that you can talk to her after school and get things straightened out. But the truth is, Kyle, that quite often there will be something or someone that can cause us to become distracted if we allow them to. At some point, we all have to learn how to temporarily put those things aside so that we can pay attention to what is important in the present. And right now, Kyle, what's important is you finishing your assignment. Take a deep breath and try to clear your mind. Then we'll go back in the room and you can concentrate on what you're learning in this class. You'll have to turn the assignment in at the end of class."

"Not only will I turn it in on time," Kyle began, "but I will make sure that I do my absolute best on it."

Kyle's teacher looked a little skeptical, but she nodded her head and said, "That's good to hear. Kyle, give this thing with Kaitlin a little time. The two of you are such good friends that you will be able to work through whatever it was that you were fighting about."

"Thanks, Mrs. B.," he said, "I sure hope so."

With that, he followed her into the classroom and took his seat. His buddy Allan was sitting in the desk next to his. Kyle sat down and pulled his paper toward him with the intention of focusing on nothing but his assignment. Just as Kyle was about to start writing an answer on his paper, Allan leaned over and teased him, saying, "Oooohhh, Kyle, what happened? I saw the teacher take you out in the hallway. Did you get in trouble? What did you do wrong?"

Kyle, who didn't feel like getting into more trouble, glared at Allan and said, "I got scolded for spacing out and not doing my assignment. I'm trying very hard to get this done, but now you're distracting me again."

"Touchy today, aren't we?" Allan teased. "I noticed that you didn't ride the bus today. I also noticed that Kaitlin was awfully quiet. Did you two get into a fight?"

"Yeah, kind of," Kyle volunteered. "But I'll work it out with her. She's my . . ." Kyle trailed off when he realized that he was about to tell Allan that Kaitlin was his best friend.

Allan, Kyle realized, thought of himself as Kyle's best friend. Kyle didn't want to hurt Allan's feelings, but he also realized that even though it was true that there was no friend that was closer than Kaitlin, Allan would never understand that.

"Were you going to say that Kaitlin is your *girlfriend*?" Allan asked, seizing on the chance to get a dig in at Kyle. He continued, "I've wondered about that. You two do spend a whole lot of time together."

"Of course we do!" Kyle retorted. "We've been neighbors since I was born." He stole a quick glance at his teacher, who didn't seem to notice the exchange between the two boys. He turned his attention back to Allan and said, "Now, you've got to leave me alone. I have to finish this assignment, or I really will be in trouble!"

"Yep, just like I said before," Allan said, "you're awfully touchy. You better talk to Kaitlin later or you're going to be in a bad mood for days!"

Kyle didn't want to admit it, but what Allan was saying probably had some truth to it. Even he could hear the edge in his words. With that thought in mind he replied, "I will talk to her later."

Allan seemed to be satisfied by this and turned back to the paper on his desk. Kyle did the same and finished his assignment with only a minute left on the clock before the bell rang. He threw his books back into his pack and walked up to the teacher's desk to hand in his assignment.

"On time as promised, Mrs. B.," he said with a forced smile.

"That's good, Kyle," she responded. "How about tomorrow we see if you can come in here with your focus solely on your lessons?"

"I'll do my best," Kyle promised. With that, he was off to his next class.

The rest of the day he forced himself to concentrate on what he was supposed to be learning. His talk with Mrs. B. had been an eye-opener. He had realized that he wasn't doing himself any favors by allowing himself to dwell on something that he couldn't fix right now. In his gym class at the end of the day, he decided that even though he had time to take a shower, he wasn't going to bother.

Go figure, he thought. *The one day I don't have to worry about missing the bus and I don't even want to take a shower.* Taking a shower now seemed like it would be pointless given that he was going to be riding his bike to the cave and then home again. The hot sun would be beating down on him while he was riding, which would cause him to sweat. And then he would be in the cave, where he would certainly get dirty. *No,* he reassured himself, *I definitely don't want to take a shower!*

Kyle exited the front doors of the school and walked out to his bike. He needed to unlock the bike, so he threw his backpack on the ground next to him. It landed with a loud "thump," which puzzled Kyle. He had forgotten that not only did he have his textbooks in there, but he had also brought some things with him for use in the cave.

"Oh, rats!" he said as he thought about the contents of his backpack. He riffled through the pack and dug to the bottom where he had placed his water bottle this morning. He thought about what a mess it would make if it had broken and was leaking all over his homework. Kyle's hand traveled around in the backpack until it found the water bottle. "Whew!" Kyle said to himself. "It doesn't appear to be leaking anywhere."

With that potential disaster averted, he proceeded to look for the flashlight that he would need in the cave. It too seemed to be intact, so he closed the zipper on the pack and slung it over his shoulders. He finished unlocking the bike and pulled it out of the rack. Before he knew it, he was on his way to the beach.

Two thoughts occurred to Kyle on his journey. The first was that leaving from the school made for a much shorter trip than it would have been from his house. That, he thought, would give him a little more time for exploring. Overall, he thought that riding his bike to school today had been a good decision. Unfortunately, that meant there was no chance that he could try to talk Kaitlin into coming with him. She was the second thing that had been on his mind during the ride to the cave. How he wished that she was going with him! His enjoyment of his time at the cave would be somewhat tempered by the fact that Kaitlin wasn't there. *If only those men wouldn't have shown up yesterday!* he fumed to himself. He could feel frustration bubbling under the surface of his emotions. He realized that more than the fear of running into Colonel Kentucky and his sidekick was that he would never be able to get Kaitlin to come back to the cave.

His thoughts had caused him to lose track of his surroundings, and before he knew it, he was pulling into the parking lot at the beach. Once again, he locked his bike up and headed out on the path that led to the cave.

Typically, he chose to take the path that was visible from the beach because it seemed to him that it would be less conspicuous to other visitors to the beach. Today, though, he decided that it really didn't matter what other people saw or thought. All he wanted was to get into that cave as fast as he could. By going through the back entrance, he would be able to avoid going through a lot of the rooms that he had been through so many times before.

So Kyle headed up the path on the back side of the beach wall, lugging his backpack with him. He walked steadily upward as quickly as he could until he came to the hole that allowed him to enter the cave. Before he crawled through the opening, he scanned the area to see if there was anyone lurking about. As there was no sign of a living being in sight, he proceeded into the darkness of the tunnel.

The backpack felt extremely heavy to be hauling around in the cave, especially now when he was crawling. He concluded that he really didn't have a choice in the matter, though, considering that if he would have left his backpack with his bike, it could easily have been snatched. He chuckled a little to himself as he thought that he wouldn't be too disappointed if his textbooks and homework were to disappear. His grin grew bigger as he pictured himself trying to explain to his teachers what had happened to his books.

I have a feeling they would be more likely to believe that my dog ate my homework than they would believe that my backpack was stolen, he said to himself. He pictured the imaginary would-be thief snatching the pack thinking that they were going to find some toys or snorkeling gear for the beach. *Wouldn't they be in for a surprise,* Kyle thought, *if they opened the zipper, only to find a bunch of books and papers.* The image was so amusing that he almost laughed out loud. Kyle thought better of it and bit his lip to keep the laughter in. After all, he still wasn't a hundred percent sure that those men weren't hanging around here somewhere. He didn't want to make it easy for them to find him if they *were* here.

Kyle finally entered the room at the end of the tunnel. *Which way shall I go today?* he asked himself. He switched on his flashlight and swept the beam to the right first. It occurred to him that he and Kaitlin had come from that direction yesterday, and truthfully there wasn't much to see in that room. *As a matter of fact,* he reminded himself, *there isn't much of anything in any of the rooms that we went through yesterday. I guess if our time had to be cut short, I'm thankful we weren't in a room I'd never been in before.* With that thought in mind, he was certain he needed to go in a different direction. The difficulty was that this room had quite a few different passages to choose from. He was having a very hard time deciding which way might lead him to an "exciting" room. In his mind, exciting meant that it would have some aspect that he had not yet come across in this cave.

There were three other entrances that he could choose from. One was off to the far left of the room. The other two were right next to each other in the center of the far wall of the cave. Kyle directed the beam of the flashlight at those two entrances and concluded that one of them would be where he would begin his exploration today.

Now, how am I going to pick which one to go through? Kyle asked himself. He shone the flashlight down the tunnel on the left first. He couldn't really see much, other than a few stalactites hanging from the ceiling. *Well,* Kyle thought, *I didn't see anything that really caught my attention, so I'll check out the other one.* As the flashlight's beam penetrated the darkness, Kyle wasn't sure that this way would be any better than the one next to it. But just as he was about to direct the beam back to the spot where he stood, the light reflected off of something in the tunnel that made him stop in his tracks. He moved the flashlight around to get a better look at whatever it was, but from where he stood, he was unable to figure out what the thing was. However, the glimpse of whatever it was solidified in his mind that it was that tunnel that he would start in.

Kyle directed the flashlight through the tunnel once more to see if he could figure out what it was that he had seen. His curiosity was so strong that he searched every square inch that was within his line of sight. Try as he might, though, he couldn't find it. He stood there trying to figure out the puzzle of the disappearing "thing." He re-played the scene in his mind and it dawned on him that he may have seen it, not when the light was shining on it, but after he had swept the beam back into his own room. He stepped closer to the entrance and shone the flashlight inside the tunnel. Again, he could see nothing. The mystery of the "thing" was getting the better of him, so he turned the light off and stepped even nearer to the entrance. This time he detected a glimmer in the far reaches of his line of sight. He still had no idea what it was, but now he was absolutely certain that he needed to go this way.

As he first entered the tunnel, he realized that he was able to fully stand, and that meant that there would be no crawling on his hands and knees. Kyle had to admit to himself that he was relieved. After all, if he were to encounter anyone in here, he would have a much better chance of outmaneuvering them if he were able to run instead of crawl. He had switched the flashlight on again to get his bearings in the tunnel. His plan was to follow the tunnel to about the spot where he saw the "thing" and then turn the light off again. If his theory was correct, he wasn't going to see it at all with the light on.

Kyle moved forward until he reached the spot where he was fairly certain he had seen it. He shone the beam of the flashlight further down the tunnel and noticed that it had almost a zigzag pattern. *I'm going to have to get a good look at that again before I continue any further,* he told himself. He studied it a bit longer and saw that the tunnel veered first to the right, then to the left, and further in it appeared to turn to the right again. Although he couldn't explain why, Kyle had a feeling deep in the pit of his stomach that this was going to be a great day of exploring.

He pushed the button to switch the light off and stood still to allow his eyes time to get used to the darkness. In his mind, he tried to picture the layout of the tunnel ahead of him. "Nuts!" he said, and then he chided himself, saying, "I should have gotten a better feel for the distances between the turns!" He sighed heavily, and then reassured himself that he could always turn the light on once again before he continued on. With that settled, he scanned the tunnel, but his vision was still adjusting to the darkness.

Kyle had learned that if one or more of his senses were not working to their full potential, it heightened the other senses. In essence, they allowed the person to experience their surroundings in a different way. Kyle's eyes were temporarily closed so that he could see nothing but the backs of his eyelids. However, in this very moment, he found out how true what he had learned about his other senses taking over was. With his nose, he was able to detect a faint hint of moisture in the air. The smell was similar to that of an overcast day in which rain is just about to burst forth from the clouds. He was also able to determine that there was a somewhat musty smell. It reminded him of being down in his basement after ground water had found its way in through the cracks of the house's foundation.

Kyle heard a distant dripping sound, but it seemed to be quite a bit further ahead in the tunnel. Other than that, Kyle could hear nothing. *Good,* he thought, *that means no one is coming after me!* He allowed himself to open his eyes. At first, it seemed as if the tunnel was as pitch-black as it had been before he closed them. However, after a few seconds of adjusting, he found that he was actually able to see quite well. He scanned every inch of the walls next to him and behind him and didn't see anything that appeared to be out of the ordinary. "Oh, come on," he said excitedly. "I know I saw something! Where on earth is it?" He looked them over once more and still saw nothing. In his frustration, he was about to give up when he realized that he had not inspected the ceiling above him.

Kyle turned his eyes upward and, lo and behold, there it was. He found it hard to describe the "thing" to himself, and he had no idea how he would describe it to Kaitlin when he told her about it. All he did know, right in this moment, was that what he saw above him was mesmerizing. There was a bluish-green glow emanating from the "thing." At first, he assumed it was some kind of glowing moss that was growing on the rock. However, unless his eyes were playing tricks on him, he would have sworn that he saw the glow *move.* He watched it for some time to see if it would move again, but he saw nothing. *I must have imagined it,* Kyle told himself. *My eyes are playing tricks on me.* He looked at the glow once more, just to be sure it wasn't going to move again. But there was not even a hint of movement. He shrugged his shoulders and figured that since he couldn't figure out the mystery of the "thing" he might as well turn the flashlight back on. He reasoned that at some point he would have to keep moving forward.

Kyle flicked his light back on and really examined the layout of the tunnel ahead. This time he was careful to estimate the distance between his current spot and where the next turn was. He approximated that he had about ten feet to go before he reached the first right turn. The second turn was a little harder to determine, but based on what he could see, it appeared that there was a distance of about twelve feet from the right turn to where the tunnel veered to the left. The last right turn was much too far back for him to figure out a distance. *At least not yet,* Kyle thought.

He took one last look at the tunnel, trying to memorize the pattern of the tunnel's direction. It was almost as if he was trying to take a snapshot of it with his mind. Kyle turned off the light once again and allowed his eyes time to readjust to the darkness. The glow was still there, and as far as he could tell, it still had not moved. Kyle tentatively took one step forward with his right foot.

When he had first begun his cave explorations, he had come up with a method to determine approximate distances that he was traveling. He had gotten the idea from movies he had watched with his parents, which showed the individual counting out paces until they reached their destination. When he had first attempted the process, he came to the conclusion that the single pace of an adult's step was probably bigger than his own. His paces hadn't quite worked out as well as they appeared to in the movies. Over time, however, he had learned that because he wasn't a full-grown adult, his stride pattern probably meant one and a half paces equaled a full foot.

With this concept in mind, Kyle began counting out his paces. He had started with his right foot and made a full pace. Then he would follow with his left foot, only this time moving half the distance. He repeated the process until he counted out enough paces to reach the turn. With his hand, he reached out and felt along the wall of the tunnel. It turned out that his calculations had been almost spot on. He could tell by the feel of the wall that he had just a few inches to go before he reached the portion of the tunnel that turned right. He slid forward slightly, not wanting to throw off his original calculations. As he rounded the corner, he began the process of counting out his strides again. Kyle counted his sixth stride, approximating that he was halfway to the distance where the tunnel turned left. However, as he was swinging his foot forward to make another pace, he noticed that the tunnel appeared to be getting brighter.

Kyle looked at the ceiling above him and saw that there were quite a few more of the glowing "things." As a matter of fact, they were not only on the ceiling, but as he went farther into the tunnel, he noticed that they were also attached at the top of the walls. He watched the glowing things and this time there was no denying that they were moving.

"What on earth?" Kyle said in disbelief. The glowing "things," it appeared, were actually alive. This notion propelled Kyle on, causing him to move much faster than he had been up until this point. Any thought of precautionary measures seemed to be forgotten in his haste to get to the next room. He counted out seven more paces, but quickly realized his mistake when he smacked right into the wall. "OW!" yelped a startled Kyle. His right shoulder had taken the brunt of the impact, so he rubbed it vigorously until the throbbing started to subside. Once it did, he stared up at the mysterious little creatures that seemed to be multiplying with every step he took.

He forced himself to turn on his flashlight once again to get a better view of the tunnel as it veered off to the right. Upon doing so, he noticed that the tunnel came to an end and opened out into an enormous room. As of yet, Kyle had not come across a room quite this large in his explorations. He could see that there were pools of various sizes throughout the room and realized that this would make it absolutely necessary for him to tread cautiously. He took a good look around to try to get a feel for the placement of the pools. Once he felt as if he had the room fairly memorized, he shut off the flashlight again.

Kyle took his first few steps slowly because he remembered that a pool lay almost directly ahead of him. He stopped at this point and scanned the perimeter of the room. The glowing "things" were everywhere now. It seemed to Kyle that almost every square inch of the room was covered with the little critters, from the floor to the highest point of the ceiling. He threw his head back and stared and uttered the only word that he could think of: "WOW!" In his silent reverie, Kyle had not heard the footsteps of a person approaching him. He was completely lost in the moment, staring above and all around him. "Wow is right!" he heard a female voice say. "What are they?"

"Who's there?" Kyle nearly shrieked.

He heard a familiar-sounding giggle followed by, "It's just me, silly!"

"Kaitlin? Is that you?" he asked, still sounding on the verge of being terrified.

Kaitlin laughed again and said, "Yes, it's me."

"Well, how . . . I mean, I came in here by myself . . . I mean, you said you weren't going to come with me today . . . How did you find me anyway?" Kyle asked in a steady stream of jumbled thoughts.

"Hmmm," Kaitlin began, "well, it turned out that right after I saw you take off on your bike this morning I started feeling guilty. I thought about how excited you had been to show me this place.

Then I realized that your hopes had been completely dashed when we had to leave so quickly." She paused for a few seconds and then continued, "And then dumb old me went and vowed that I would never set foot in this cave again. On the bus ride to school I realized how much that had to have hurt you. So, this afternoon, on the way home, I made up my mind that as soon as I got home I would hop on my bike and follow you here."

"Thanks, Kaitlin!" was all that a very surprised Kyle could come up with. He thought about her trip to the cave, and asked, "So, which way did you come in?"

"I came in the way we did yesterday," Kaitlin responded.

"And you didn't see anyone lurking around out there?" Kyle prodded.

"Nope. No one," Kaitlin reassured him.

Kyle took a deep breath and blew it out slowly. It was the first time he felt as if he could breathe since Kaitlin had startled him. Kyle was still feeling a bit shaken up, so he asked Kaitlin, "You're absolutely sure that you didn't see *anyone* outside before you came in, right?"

"Yes, Kyle," Kaitlin soothed. "You know me, if I would have seen even a hint of someone being out there, I would have shouted for you to run, and I would have taken off!"

Kyle laughed slightly and nodded his head in agreement. "You would have, wouldn't you?" he said as he smiled at her.

"Yep!" Kaitlin agreed. "Although, if you didn't respond, I may have come in here to make sure that you would leave."

"That'll be the day!" Kyle said mockingly.

"Hey," Kaitlin retorted, "I'm here now, aren't I?"

"Yes. Yes, you are," Kyle agreed.

They both turned to look at the glowing lights all around them.

"Kyle," Kaitlin said, "you never told me what those things are."

Kyle turned to look at his friend and answered, "Kaitlin, if I had even the slightest idea what they were, I would be glad to tell you."

The young friends stood there in the silence, staring at the luminescent little creatures in awe. Kaitlin was just about to open her mouth to ask another question when they heard a strange male voice say, "Those, my dear young lady, are *Arachnocampa luminosa.*"

CHAPTER 13

K aitlin stood there, frozen. She stared at Kyle and saw that his eyes looked as if they were going to pop out of his head. She had a flashback of cartoons that she had watched when she was younger. She could envision the character with his eyes bugging way out, hanging by only the roots of the eyeballs. The sound effect they had used sounded like a very old car horn that said, "Ah-ooga." If the circumstances had been different, she may have laughed long and hard at the expression on his face. Unfortunately, she realized, this was not a cartoon, and Kyle looked very scared. That made her feel even more afraid.

"Kyle," she began in a shaky voice, "please tell me that was you!"

Kyle did not respond for what seemed like forever and continued to stare straight ahead. His mouth was open, as if he was trying to say something but just couldn't get the words out.

Then Kaitlin heard a voice from behind her say, "No, Miss Kaitlin, it was not Kyle. It was me."

In spite of her fear, Kaitlin recognized that the voice belonged to a man with a very heavy German accent. In the silence, she could tell that the man was approaching the two of them by the sound of his footsteps. Her heart began to beat wildly, as if it were going to jump out of her chest. Her imagination took hold of her as she pictured the man grabbing the two of them and hauling them off to one of the deepest rooms in the cave. The footsteps grew ever closer to her, and she was certain that the man was going to catch her by the arm and hold her prisoner. Instead, he walked past her and stood between Kyle and her. When she saw his face, she recognized the older man that she had seen at the church.

Kyle finally seemed to come out of his trance and blurted out, "Colonel Ken—" but that was all the farther he got. The man in front of them burst into laughter, so loud that it echoed around the walls of the cave. Kyle and Kaitlin watched and waited to see what he would do next. However, he really didn't *do* anything. When he had finally finished his fit of laughter, he said, "Oh, children, I get that all the time! I have never even seen this Colonel Kentucky, but everywhere I travel, people think that I am him."

Kyle, who had his cell phone with him, pulled it out of his pocket and began a frantic search on the Internet. Within a minute, he had found a commercial for the restaurant, which portrayed the owner sitting at a table outside of his restaurant with some of his customers. He was seated next to a family of four and was holding a piece of deep-fried chicken in his hand. He slowly brought the piece of chicken up to his mouth, took a bite, and proclaimed, "Mmmm, mmm, lip-smackin' good!"

The man watched in interest until the commercial was finished and then he said, "Well, I certainly can see the resemblance, but the two of us sound *nothing* alike!"

Kyle broke into a grin and said, "You can say that again!"

The man looked confused, opened his mouth, and began to repeat, "We sound nothing al—"

Kyle interrupted him and said, "You're not from around here, are you? That is an expression people use to tell someone that they are very much in agreement with what they are saying."

The man took a brief pause to ponder this new information and then smiled. "Indeed," he said, "I am still learning about the language and culture here." He stuck his hand out to Kyle, and with a smile that could have lit up the room all by itself, he said, "Allow me to introduce myself. My name is Heinrich Von Lichtenspiel."

"Von Lichten . . . what?" asked Kaitlin.

"Von Lichtenspiel," the man repeated. "I hail from Deutschland." When neither Kyle nor Kaitlin responded, the man realized that they were not aware of what he was speaking of. "Deutschland is the given name for the land that I come from," he explained. "You may know it better as Germany."

Both Kyle and Kaitlin nodded and replied, "Oh!"

Seeing that they were less guarded than they had previously been, the man continued, *"Ja,* I am a professor at the university in my hometown. I teach students the studies of rocks and bones and ancient civilizations . . ."

Kyle interrupted him and excitedly said, "You teach archaeology!" He turned to Kaitlin and said, "Now it all makes sense."

Kaitlin still wasn't completely sure about the intentions of the man standing in front of them. However, she had to admit to herself that he did not seem to be the type to go around kidnapping children from a cave. She turned to address "V. L." as she had already nicknamed him, because to her it seemed much too difficult to pronounce his name. "So, if you are a professor in Germany, what are you doing here?"

"Well," he answered in a measured tone, "as I said, I am a professor of archaeology. I have taught this subject for many, many years."

Kyle interrupted and asked, "How many years is many?"

The professor chuckled a bit and answered, "Since well before you were born, young Kyle." He winked at Kyle and continued, "In case you wonder, I am sixty-eight years of age."

"WOW!" Kaitlin interjected. "You're older than my grandfather!"

The professor erupted into a fit of laughter. When he was finally able to catch his breath, he said, "*Ja*, Miss Kaitlin, but you will find that I am very spry for a man of my age."

Kyle, who was becoming impatient to hear the rest of the man's story, said, "So, you taught archaeology in Germany? How did you end up here? What made you fly across the world to come to this particular cave?"

"Forgive me," the professor replied, "I forget myself sometimes." He appeared to be trying to remember where he had left off before. "Oh, *ja*," he began. "As I said, I have taught the study of archaeology for many years. I would often hear stories of my fellow professors who had gone on expeditions and tripped upon great historical finds."

"He means 'stumbled,'" Kaitlin interjected.

"I knew what he meant!" Kyle said in a huff. "Let the man finish!"

Kaitlin looked at the professor humbly and said, "I apologize, V... I mean, Professor. Please continue."

The professor nodded and continued, "Well, many years had gone by, and I had not found my one great discovery. I had been on several small expeditions, but the truth is, they hit bottom."

"He means they fell flat," Kaitlin interrupted.

"Kaitlin, I know that!" Kyle said in exasperation. "Please let him talk." Kaitlin pursed her lips and said nothing, and Kyle said, "Please continue, Professor."

"Certainly, I speak too much," the professor answered. "I only want you both to understand that I mean you no harm. I explain my story so that you know why I am here." He paused, waited to see if either of the two had any questions, and then continued. "Finally, about a year ago, an old friend of mine came to pay me a visit. He told me of a story that he had heard from many different professors and archaeologists alike. Apparently, this story has been told for thousands of years and passed from one generation to another. Not only has the story been passed out to the people of Germany . . ."

Kyle glanced over at Kaitlin. He was sure she was about to interrupt and say, "He means passed on." But Kaitlin caught his look of warning and clamped her mouth shut.

" . . . but apparently, it has been told in many other countries as well," the professor concluded.

"What story is that, Professor Von Lichtenspiegel?" Kyle asked with sincere interest. He caught a slight smile from the professor but was unaware that he had mispronounced the professor's name. "I have been interested in archaeology since I was a little boy, and I have never heard any fascinating stories about caves. I've only learned what I've read in my books. And they sure don't have any great stories to tell. Great pictures, yes, but *not* great stories."

"*Ja*, young Kyle, this story has been passed down only to those who truly seek treasure. But not just any treasure, you know. It is the kind of treasure that only those with open hearts wish to find. You, Kyle, I believe, are a young man with an open heart. So *ja*, I will share this story with you."

"Thank you, Professor," Kyle said and smiled. Then he added, "You said this story involves treasure that only those with open hearts would seek. So, what kind of treasure is this?"

The professor's face grew serious and he answered, "The legend has it that—"

Just then the loud rumbling noise of a dirt bike came from outside the cave and the professor stopped what he was saying to listen intently.

Kyle and Kaitlin both had a look of fear on their faces. To them, the sound was that of an unwelcome intruder. Kaitlin had a flashback of the day Kyle's shed had been broken into. She pictured the man with the black sweat suit and the ski mask. She could recall him hiding behind Kyle's shed and she also remembered hearing Chester bark in the background. She replayed the image in her mind of Kyle being knocked in the head with the shed door. Just then she looked up and saw Kyle rubbing his forehead, as if he, too, were recalling that very moment. Kaitlin swung her gaze over in the direction of the professor. *Kyle was right*, she thought. *We have nothing to be afraid of with him. It's the other guy that I'm worried about.* As she watched the expression on Kyle's face, it became apparent to her that her fear of the other man was shared by Kyle.

"Ah, that will be Anthony!" the professor said with great enthusiasm.

"Who is *Anthony*?" Kyle asked with a hint of worry in his voice. Kyle looked over at Kaitlin, and it appeared to him that she was ready to take off running at the slightest hint of danger. Kyle gave Kaitlin a look as if to say, "Not yet. Don't run yet."

The professor answered Kyle's question. "Oh, Anthony? He is my nephew. I understand that you had a meeting with him the other day."

"A *meeting?!*" Kaitlin exclaimed. "I wouldn't exactly call that a meeting!"

"Well, you were introduced to him, were you not?" the professor asked her.

"That was no introduction!" Kaitlin retorted. "He was trying to steal something from Kyle and he hit Kyle on the head!"

"Ah, pish-posh!" the professor responded. "My nephew would not hurt a flea!"

"A fly?" Kaitlin asked, and smiled a bit in spite of herself.

The professor smiled as well and said, "Yes, a fly. I get those two confused often."

Kyle jumped into the conversation and asked, "If he wasn't trying to hurt me, and he wasn't trying to steal from me, what was he doing in my shed?"

The professor appeared to be about to answer, but then Kyle noticed that the professor's gaze shifted. He watched as the professor's eyes swung in the direction of the man with dark hair.

Anthony, who now stood to the right of the professor, said, "Hello, Uncle." Then Anthony turned to Kyle and responded, "I was in there because I had to see for myself if you had found it."

"Found what?" Kyle asked, but Kaitlin had spoken at the same time.

"Hey, wait a minute," she said. "Professor, you are from Germany, but Anthony looks as if he is from Italy. How is it, then, that he can be your nephew?"

The professor considered her question and then answered, "You are very perceptive, Miss Kaitlin."

Kaitlin's eyes grew wide at the statement, as if she expected to find out that the professor had been lying to them this whole time. This time, instead of the professor being the one to drag them away, it was Anthony whom Kaitlin envisioned putting them into a makeshift prison.

The professor saw the look of panic that had crossed her face, saw the same look reflected on Kyle's face, and quickly said, "Ach! There is nothing to fret over, young ones! Anthony Rigotelli is indeed my nephew and—"

"Rigotelli, like the pasta?" Kaitlin asked.

Kyle burst out in laughter and said, "Gee whiz, Kaitlin, that's rigatoni!"

Kaitlin laughed at herself as well, and then made a joke out of the name. "Anthony Pasta! Did the kids ever call you Anti-pasto in school?"

"Hardy, har, har!" Anthony replied.

The professor reined in the conversation once again, saying, "Anthony's mother is my sister. She married a man from Italy and I very rarely saw her after that. One day, Anthony here showed up in my office at the university and informed me that he was my nephew. He told me details about my sister that no one who was not family could know. Then," he said with a deeply saddened voice, "he told me that my sister had perished." The professor paused to wipe a stray tear off of his cheek. After collecting himself he continued, "Anthony's father had left when he was much younger. So, as it turns out, I am the only family that he has left, and he is the only family that I have left."

Kaitlin, never one who liked to see people cry, tried to distract the professor from the sad memories. "Professor V., what was it that you said those glowing things are called? Arachno . . .?"

The professor seemed to perk up a bit as he could focus on a subject he was familiar with. He answered, "Arachnocampa luminosa."

"They're beautiful," Kaitlin said, looking in awe at the glowing lights all around the cave. The rest of them remained silent for a few moments, looking on in wonder at the spectacle before their eyes. "They remind me of the night sky full of stars," Kaitlin said, in an almost dreamlike state.

"I thought the same thing when I first saw them, Kaitlin," Kyle agreed. "But, Professor, what *are* they?"

"Very interesting question, Kyle," the professor responded. "The name means 'spider-worm, glowing,'" he began.

"Spider-worm?" Kaitlin asked and shuddered. "I'm out of here!"

Kyle grabbed hold of her arm and whispered, "Not yet. We'll leave together. Besides, I want to hear about these things."

Kaitlin shrugged and whispered back, "Fine, but this better be quick. Those things are giving me the creeps!"

"That's funny," Kyle teased, "a minute ago you thought they looked like beautiful stars."

"Hmmph!" was all Kaitlin said in response.

In the meantime, the professor had continued his story, " . . . in this form for a short time. Truly, they are what you call, hmm . . . it starts with an 'm.'"

"Mosquito?" Kyle asked.

"Well, yes," the professor agreed, "very similar to that. But while they are still larvae, they have a glowing light in their posterior . . ."

"He means their rear end," Kaitlin interjected.

"I know that!" Kyle said vehemently. "Let him finish!"

"Sorry, Professor," Kaitlin said. "Please keep going. I want to know about the icky spider-worms."

The professor chuckled a bit and said, "Alas for the poor Arachnocampa, it seems that once people find out what they are, they have the same reaction as Miss Kaitlin here. They are quite fascinating, though, if you take the time to study them. They use their glowing 'rear end' as you say to attract their prey. They spin webs like a spider to catch insects, just like a spider does, which is how they got their name."

Kyle found himself staring at the glowing little creatures that covered the walls and the ceiling of the entire room. He pulled out his phone to take a picture of the scene before him. After he finished, he looked at the time on his phone.

"OH NO!" he shouted out into the semi-silent room.

"Ruh-roh, Raggy!" Kaitlin said, as she mimicked Scooby Doo. "You're going to get it if you don't get home before your mom does!"

"You're right!" Kyle said. He grabbed Kaitlin's hand and they began to head toward the cave's rear exit. Kyle turned and addressed the professor's nephew. "Anthony, what did you mean when you said you wanted to know if I 'found it'?"

"Not now!" Kaitlin said. This time *she* grabbed Kyle's hand and they started running.

Kyle looked over his shoulder one more time and said, "See you next time, Professor!"

As they got on their bikes to make their way home, Kyle suddenly threw on the brakes.

"What's wrong?" Kaitlin asked in a panicked voice.

"Kaitlin," Kyle said breathlessly, "he knew our names!"

CHAPTER 14

"**S**o, he knew our names," Kaitlin said in an exasperated voice. "What's the big deal?"

Kyle looked her right in the eyes and said in a measured tone, "I didn't tell him my name. Did you?"

Kaitlin paused to think about this new information. In truth, she had a difficult time remembering the entire experience. It seemed that so much had happened in such a short amount of time.

She recalled the professor coming up and standing between the two of them and his story about the legend that he had heard from one of his archaeologist friends. Then, as her mind replayed the scene in the cave, she recalled Anthony being in the room with them and the professor's story about Anthony being his nephew and his sister's passing. Finally, she recalled the professor's explanation of what the glowing lights in the cave actually were. She shuddered a little as she thought again that they were "spider-worms." She had to admit to herself, *They are beautiful, though.* However, try as she might to remember a time when the professor had asked for their names, she could not. He had introduced *himself*, but he had not asked for their names.

Kaitlin answered, "No, Kyle, I never told him my name. And I don't remember you telling him yours either."

"See!" Kyle exclaimed. "I told you! This is kind of creepy. I still don't feel like we need to worry about him; at least not too much. But how could he possibly know our names if he didn't ask us?"

"Well," Kaitlin said slowly, as if she were pondering the possibilities, "maybe he went to the school and found out our names there."

"No way!" Kyle shouted. "The school would never give out that information!"

"You're right about that," Kaitlin responded. She continued, "Then maybe he ... well, he could have ... Aw, nuts! I don't know."

Kyle could see that her mind was racing with possibilities, so he gave her a minute to come up with another explanation.

"I've got it!" Kaitlin all but shrieked. "He must have been following us around near the cave and heard us calling each other by our names!"

"Hmm," Kyle said thoughtfully, "that does kind of make sense. There isn't anyone else around here that knows we've been exploring the cave, so the professor would not be able to ask someone what our names are without giving away that he is interested in the cave." Kyle paused for a moment and then added, "Yes, Kaitlin, you must be right. If he asked someone in town, then he would have to explain about the cave. And he doesn't want anyone snooping around that cave any more than we do."

"OK," Kaitlin said, "now we've got that settled. I mean, the only other living soul that knows anything about us visiting that cave is Chester. I'm pretty sure we don't have to worry about *him* talking," she said with a wink and a laugh.

Kyle smiled. "I suppose you're right." He looked at the path that led to the cave once more and said, "All right, we better go. I sure don't want to risk being late."

Kyle and Kaitlin made their way home, each lost in their own thoughts. When they each pulled up in their own driveway, Kaitlin waved at Kyle and asked, "Are you going back to the cave tomorrow?"

Kyle's face lit up and he enthusiastically replied, "You betcha!"

"Great!" Kaitlin replied.

Kyle looked at her as she was responding and marveled at how much her attitude toward the cave had changed. To him it seemed that she was just as excited about it as he was. He smiled to himself, and heard her continue, "How about if we both ride our bikes to school tomorrow and then we can skip wasting time coming home first?"

Kyle shook his head from side to side in bewilderment. Kaitlin saw his reaction and instinctively thought he was saying no.

"Well, fine, Kyle," Kaitlin huffed. "If you don't like my idea, we can just meet there!"

"Oh, for crying out loud, Kaitlin," Kyle answered in exasperation. "That is not why I was shaking my head. I'm just confused . . . and happy," he said with a smile.

Kaitlin rode her bike across her yard until she reached Kyle's driveway. "What could you possibly be confused about?" she asked, a little crossly.

Kyle couldn't resist the chance to tease her. "Well, you're a girl, Kaitlin, and you girls are *always* confusing!" he said and laughed.

Kaitlin did *not* laugh. She gave Kyle a look that said, "Watch it, buddy!" But then she relented and said, "OK, so maybe we *are* a little confusing. But we are women, so we're allowed to be a little confusing at times."

Kyle was about to reply that she wasn't a woman yet, but he realized that might not be the smartest thing in the world to say. So he bit his tongue and waited to see if she had anything else to add. As it turned out, she did.

"Kyle, why did you say you were happy?"

"I'm happy," Kyle answered, "because now I can share the cave with my best friend in the whole wide world!"

Kaitlin was speechless, which was completely foreign to her. She straddled her bike and just stared at Kyle. When she finally recovered from hearing his heartfelt declaration, she said, "Of course you can! You're stuck with me, whether you like it or not, Kyle." She started to wheel her bike back in the direction of her driveway, and then she turned around once more. "Kyle," she said.

"Yes?"

Kaitlin got a big grin on her face and teased Kyle, saying, "Just don't go around telling everyone that I'm your best friend. You might ruin my reputation with the girls!"

"You're a riot, Kaitlin. See you tomorrow," Kyle said with a wave.

****

When Kyle woke the next morning, he sensed that something was wrong. As he lay in his bed, still fighting off the sleep that he was coming out of, he heard it. The rain was pouring down so hard it sounded as if the ceiling was going to crash in on top of him. He jumped out of bed and scurried across the room to the window. He peered outside, only to have his worst suspicions confirmed. It looked as if the house was stuck right in the middle of Niagara Falls.

"Oh, come on!" Kyle fumed. "This can't be happening!"

He dressed in his usual jeans and T-shirt, mumbling as he pulled his clothes on. "Well, I guess I don't have to worry about wearing something grubby today," he said aloud. "At least I won't hear Mom make any comments about looking a little more presentable." He ran a brush through his hair and then sat down on his bed to put on his sneakers. He was so caught up in his frustration that it barely registered that his mom was calling out to him.

"Kyle, honey, Kaitlin is here. She said the two of you were going to ride your bikes to school. It's raining awfully hard out there. Would you like for me to drive you there in the car?"

"Just a minute, Mom," Kyle replied. "I'll be right down."

He took one last look in the mirror, grabbed his backpack, and headed down the stairs. When he arrived in the kitchen, Kaitlin was sitting at the table with his mom. The two of them were chatting away about a science project that Kaitlin was working on for school. He heard his mom tell Kaitlin, "That sounds like a very interesting idea, Kaitlin. Are you planning to enter your project in the Science Fair?"

"I don't think so, Mrs. Marshall," Kaitlin replied.

"I can't imagine why not," Kyle's mom said. "It seems to me that you would do very well. You may even win the competition."

"Well, the truth is, Mrs. M., I really don't have much time to put into the project. I've been very busy lately."

Kyle shot Kaitlin a look as if to say, "Don't you dare tell her why!"

Kaitlin rescued the potential problem by saying, "I've had so much homework that I haven't been able to spend a great deal of time on this project."

"Oh, I see," Mrs. Marshall said, sounding a little disappointed. "Well, then, what do you two think about me taking you to school?"

Kyle gave Kaitlin another look, and this time he was telling her, "Say no!"

Kaitlin looked back at Kyle and gave him a slight nod as if she was saying she understood. "That's OK, Mrs. M.," she responded. "We might as well just ride the bus today. Thank you for the offer, though."

Mrs. Marshall eyed her son and said, "Kyle, would you rather ride the bus?"

Kyle hesitated briefly, not wanting to say anything that might hurt her feelings. "Um, well, we might as well just ride the bus. It doesn't make sense for you to have to get soaking wet just to take us to school. I don't want you to have to go to work looking like a drowned rat."

Kaitlin, who was nibbling on a blueberry muffin that Mrs. Marshall had given her, nearly spit the muffin out of her mouth. Kyle realized the mistake in his choice of words, and said, "I didn't mean anything by it, Mom. I just didn't want you to have to go to work with your hair all frizzed out."

This time, Kaitlin, who had just recovered from his first blunder, began coughing and choking on the muffin in her mouth. Her eyes were as round as saucers, and she was shaking her head. When she was finally able to speak, she said, "What Kyle means to say, Mrs. M., is that he truly appreciates that you would give us a ride to school. He just doesn't want you to be miserable all day at work because you had to go out in this rain for us. Right, Kyle?"

Kyle fidgeted with his backpack and shifted his feet nervously before he spoke. This time, he decided, he was going to be extra careful about the words he chose. "That's right, Mom. I would feel just awful if I knew you had to sit in that air-conditioned office all day with wet clothes."

Kaitlin gave Kyle a nod of approval. *Whew,* he thought to himself.

"Well, all right then," Mrs. Marshall said. "The two of you better get going before you miss the bus. Then I'll have to take you and I really *will* go into work looking like a drowned rat." She gave Kyle a look that made him want to sink into the floor.

"I'm sorry, Mom. I didn't mean anything bad. I just speak gibberish sometimes."

"You sure do!" Kaitlin agreed.

"I understand," Kyle's mom said. She looked at Kyle, gave him a hug, and said, "I'll see you after work tonight."

"OK, love you, Mom," Kyle said.

As he headed to the door, he grabbed a blueberry muffin to take with him on the bus. He looked at Kaitlin and thought of the day when she stuffed sandwich after sandwich in her mouth. Kaitlin looked imploringly at him and smiled gleefully when he reached for another to bring for her. "Thanks, Kyle!" Kaitlin said.

They headed out the door just as the bus was pulling up to their stop. The bus was nearly a block away, so the two of them had to make a mad dash to the place where it was parked. Kyle could see the stop sign with the blinking red light on the side of the bus beginning to pull back.

"Oh, no, not again!" he shouted. The bus driver started to pull away from the curb.

"WAIT FOR US!" he heard Kaitlin shouting. He could see her arms flailing about wildly, trying to get someone's attention. Kyle wasn't sure why, but he had a feeling that his buddy Allan was sitting at the back of the bus again. Sure enough, when he looked into the back window, there stood his friend, apparently doubled over in laughter. He saw Allan turn toward the front of the bus and within a second, the bus had stopped.

When they entered the bus and finally sat down, Allan leaned over the back of their seat and mocked them. "I guess old Kyle here is rubbing off on you, hey, Kaitlin?"

"Oh, zip it, will you, Allan?" Kaitlin shot back.

"Yeah!" Renee, who was sitting in the seat across from Kaitlin, said vehemently. "Why don't you tell them how *you* almost missed the bus this morning, Allan?"

Allan looked like he had been hit in the stomach, and he slowly sat down without another word.

"Thanks, Renee," Kaitlin said.

"Any time," Renee said.

With that, Kaitlin turned her attention to Kyle to talk about the turn of the day's events. "So, we can't go to the cave today . . ." she began.

"Don't remind me!" Kyle pouted.

"How about we go get some ice cream after school?" Kaitlin asked, trying to console Kyle.

"That's fine," Kyle said, but didn't sound excited at all.

"Good," Kaitlin said, "I'll meet you there. I have something to do before we go."

****

By the time school was over and he arrived home, it appeared to Kyle that the rain was not coming down as hard as it had been that morning. His first thought was that maybe he and Kaitlin could go to the cave after all. However, he realized that when, or if, the rain stopped, there would not be enough time for he and Kaitlin to ride their bikes to the cave, do their exploring, and still make it home in time for dinner. Kyle decided that it would be best to stick to the original plan of meeting Kaitlin at the ice cream parlor. He grabbed his bike out of the garage and proceeded to ride it to the main street of town where the ice cream parlor was located. When he arrived at the store front, Kyle locked up his bike. He walked in the front door, and a bell chimed signaling his entry. Mr. Brown, the owner, approached Kyle and asked him how he was doing.

"I'm OK, Charlie," Kyle answered. "I'd like to have a malt please."

"Sure thing, Kyle," Charlie answered. "Will you be sitting at the counter today?"

"No, actually, Kaitlin is going to meet me here," Kyle said.

"Oh, good," Charlie said. "I'll find a nice booth for the two of you."

"Thank you," Kyle replied. He sat down in the booth and pulled out a math assignment to work on while he waited for Kaitlin. He was so absorbed in his homework that he didn't notice Charlie had come back to the table holding his malt.

"Here you go, Kyle," Charlie said, placing the glass on the table.

"Thank you, Charlie," Kyle said, beginning to brighten at the thought of the malt.

Charlie started to walk away, but then he paused and said, "Do you mind if I sit with you for a minute?"

"Sure, Charlie," Kyle responded. "What's new?"

"Well, kiddo, I just wanted to ask you a quick question," Mr. Brown began. "There was someone asking about you and Kaitlin about a week ago. He wanted to know all kinds of information about you two. He was describing you and Kaitlin so well, I just thought that maybe you knew him. At one point, I accidentally slipped and told him your names. Do you know the man?"

"Was he older?" Kyle asked.

Charlie smiled and answered, "I guess that's relative, but yes, you could say he was older."

"I think I know who you're talking about," Kyle responded, "but I just met him yesterday."

"Oh, Kyle, I'm sorry," Charlie said, looking worried. "I had no idea that you didn't know him."

"Charlie, it's not a problem," Kyle reassured him. "He's actually a very nice man."

"I'm thankful to hear that," Charlie said, and sighed with relief. "I've been so worried ever since I talked to him." Charlie gave Kyle a pat on the shoulder and said, "I'll be back for Kaitlin's order when she comes in."

"Sounds good, Charlie," Kyle replied.

Kyle directed his attention back to his homework, but all he could do was stare at the same math problem that he was working on before Charlie had brought him the malt. His mind was racing with the information that he had just received.

Just then, Kaitlin burst through the door with her backpack and an extra bag in her hand. "Hey, Kyle," she said. "Did you get your homework finished?"

"Um, no, I didn't," Kyle answered. "I kind of got sidetracked."

"By what?" Kaitlin asked.

"Charlie came over with my malt," Kyle began, and Kaitlin interrupted with the teasing words, "Oh, now I get it. The malt was so good you couldn't concentrate on anything else."

"No!" Kyle huffed. "Charlie sat down and talked with me for a few minutes. You're never going to believe what he told me!"

"I want to hear what he said," Kaitlin began, "but I have something for you first."

That statement grabbed Kyle's attention. He watched as Kaitlin leaned over and opened the bag she had brought with her. Ever so slowly, she pulled out a rectangular object that looked familiar to Kyle. As his eyes focused in on it, he realized that it was his treasure chest.

"Kaitlin!" Kyle exclaimed. Kaitlin smiled and opened her mouth to say something, but Kyle cut her off before she could. "Why did you bring that here?"

"Wha . . . I'm confused, Kyle!" Kaitlin said in a startled voice. "I thought you would be happy that I brought it. I figured now that we have met the colonel . . . I mean the professor, we wouldn't have to hide this thing anymore. I thought you would want to have it with you at home again." Kaitlin looked deflated because her surprise had, as the professor had said, "hit bottom."

Kyle saw the look on Kaitlin's face and apologized for his severe reaction. "Kaitlin, I'm sorry. I am glad to have the chest back, truly. And yes, we have met the professor and Anthony, and we shouldn't have to worry about them. What I don't want is for everyone who is in the parlor to see what I have. There would be too many questions."

Kaitlin pondered this information for a moment and replied, "I understand that, Kyle. I guess I didn't think it through well enough. I was just so excited to give it back to you."

"I know," Kyle reassured her. "It will be OK, Kaitlin. There aren't that many people in here now anyway." Kyle slowly opened the chest and peeked inside. The tissue was still covering the tooth and the key. He had to make sure they were still inside, so he pulled the tissue out and saw that they were safe and sound. He quickly replaced them and shut the lid.

"So, what was it that you wanted to tell me?" Kaitlin asked.

"Hmmm?" Kyle said, absently.

"You were going to tell me something when I first came in," Kaitlin reminded him. "You said that I wasn't going to believe it."

Kyle shook his head as if to clear his mind from a fog. "Right. That . . ." he began. "Well, Charlie sat down in the booth with me for a minute and he told me that about a week ago someone was asking about the two of us."

"What?" Kaitlin shrieked. "Who was it?"

"I'm pretty sure it was the professor from the way Charlie described him," Kyle answered. "Charlie said that when they were talking he accidentally told the man our names."

"Aha," Kaitlin said so loud that the others in the ice cream parlor stopped their conversations. When people resumed speaking, Kaitlin said, "Now the puzzle pieces are coming together."

Just then, Charlie approached the table. "Hello, Kaitlin," he said with a grin that could light up the sun. "What can I get for you today?"

"A malt like Kyle," Kaitlin answered.

"And I'll have another, Charlie," Kyle added.

"That's not good for you," they heard a now familiar voice say.

Kyle looked around Charlie to see the professor standing there.

"Ah, I see your friend is here now," Charlie said. "Maybe he would like to sit with you?"

"I would love to sit with them," the professor replied. "You don't mind, do you?" he asked Kyle and Kaitlin.

Kyle looked stunned at the appearance of the man that they were just talking about, but he answered, "Sure, Professor. Have a seat."

"*Danke*, Kyle," he replied with a smile.

Kyle and Kaitlin both gave him a puzzled look. "Oh, I forget myself. *Danke* means 'thank you.'"

Kaitlin nodded and smiled but she had to wonder what the professor was doing here. Was he following them everywhere they went?

"So, Kyle," the professor began, "how about we take a look at what is inside your box?"

CHAPTER 15

"**P**rofessor," Kyle began hesitantly, "I'm not so sure that's a good idea."

The professor looked puzzled. "Why on earth would you say that, Kyle?" he asked.

"Well," Kyle said, and looked around the room, "there are a lot of people here."

"*Ja!* There are," the professor agreed. "I do not see a problem with this."

"You *don't see a problem*?" Kyle asked in disbelief. "Professor, don't you think that if these people see what I have in the treasure chest, they will ask questions about where I found it?"

Professor Von Lichtenspiel looked puzzled at first, but then it became obvious to Kyle and Kaitlin that the possibilities of others discovering the artifacts were beginning to occur to the professor. The professor began to nod his head in agreement. "*Ja*, young Kyle. You are very true!"

Kyle looked at Kaitlin and saw that she was stifling a laugh. He smiled a bit in spite of the worry that he had.

Kyle looked at the professor and motioned to the treasure chest. "How about if we take this outside, Professor?" he asked. "There is a park just down the road. We could sit at a picnic table there and have at least a little bit more privacy."

Kaitlin nodded her head in agreement.

"*Ja, das ist güt!*" exclaimed the professor.

He saw the looks of confusion on the faces of Kyle and Kaitlin and reworded what he had said. "That means that this is a good idea. I am sorry. It is so easy for me to speak in my native tongue. Sometimes I forget that I am speaking with people who don't understand my language."

"That's all right, Professor," Kaitlin said. "We don't mind. Maybe you can teach us some German."

The professor's face brightened, and he said, "*Ja*, I would love to. You have learned your first phrase now. *Das ist gut* means 'This is good.' But for now, I believe we should focus on what young Kyle has in the chest."

"I agree," Kyle said. "I need to pay for my malt, and then we can leave."

Kaitlin signaled for Charlie to come to their table. When he approached, Kaitlin told him, "Charlie, Kyle needs his bill."

Charlie smiled, but refused to hand the check to Kyle. "Today your malt is on the house," he said beaming at Kyle and Kaitlin. Kyle shook his head, not wanting to accept Charlie's offer. "Please, Charlie, I would really like to pay for my malt."

"Charlie, please, we would like to pay for them!" Kyle said.

"No, Kyle," Charlie answered, "I would like to do this nice thing for you."

"Well, if that's how you really feel, Charlie," Kyle said. "We sure do appreciate it!"

Charlie smiled and said, "We will see the two of you again very soon. And maybe you will bring your friend with you as well."

"Sure thing, Charlie," Kaitlin agreed.

The three picked up their belongings and headed for the door. Once they were outside, Kyle spoke to the professor, saying, "We are riding our bikes, Professor. If you start walking down the street that way," he said, pointing, "you will see the park on the left side of the street. We will give you a head start and then meet you there."

"*Sehr güt!*" the professor responded. Again, he realized his mistake in speaking German rather than English. He looked sheepishly at the two and said, "That means 'very good.'"

"OK," Kyle said. "We will be right behind you."

The professor began walking in the direction of the park, and Kyle and Kaitlin unlocked their bikes.

While they were pulling the bikes out of the rack, Kaitlin asked Kyle, "Kyle, are you certain you want to show the professor what you have in the chest?"

"Actually, Kaitlin," Kyle began, "I was thinking about the same thing. What I've decided is that I am only going to show him the tooth. He doesn't seem to know that I have more than one thing in the chest and I would hate to give him any more information than necessary. At least, for right now."

Kaitlin nodded in agreement. "I agree," she said. "But how are we going to keep the professor from seeing the key? It's in the box with the tooth."

"Right," Kyle said with a thoughtful look on his face.

He hesitated only for a few seconds and then he opened the chest. He began to rummage around until he pulled out the wrapped key. "Kaitlin, would you mind if we put this in your backpack for now?"

"I don't mind at all," Kaitlin responded. "I think that idea is *sehr güt!*"

Kyle smiled and said, "You sure do pick up other languages quickly."

"Piece of cake!" Kaitlin said. "Speaking of cake, I'm hungry . . ."

"Oh, gee whiz, Kaitlin, you're always hungry!" Kyle teased. "Now let's put this key in your backpack and catch up with the professor."

Kaitlin took the key from Kyle's outstretched hand. She unzipped a pocket on the front of her backpack and placed the key carefully inside.

They seated themselves on their bikes and rode off in the direction of the park. By the time they arrived there, they saw that the professor had found his way to a picnic table in the shade. Kyle glanced around and noticed that there were very few people in that area of the park. Two boys he recognized from school were kicking a soccer ball around. The good thing was that Kyle was not very close to them, so he wouldn't have to worry about them asking him any questions. *Besides,* he thought, *they are so wrapped up in the soccer ball, I doubt they would pay any attention to us.* There was also a young mother who had spread out her rain coat and was seated on it with her baby. The baby seemed to be mesmerized by the blades of grass that surrounded them. Kyle watched as she grabbed one blade at a time and just stared at it, as if it was the most amazing thing in the world. The mother appeared to be as fascinated by the baby as the baby was with the grass. Other than that, there were a few young kids on the swings, but none of them seemed to even notice their appearance.

"I think we're in the clear, Kaitlin," Kyle said. "It looks like the professor found a nice private spot."

Kaitlin nodded and continued pedaling her bike in the direction of the picnic table. She wasn't as worried about the people in the park as Kyle seemed to be. Instead, she was more concerned that the professor might discover that Kyle had found more than the tooth. She determined that she would do everything she could to distract the professor if the subject were to come up.

The professor saw them approaching and waved them over. "Will this do, young Kyle?" the professor asked.

Kyle nodded and said, "Yes, Professor, I think this will work very well."

Kyle and Kaitlin dismounted from their bikes and sat across the picnic table from the professor. Kyle pulled the chest from his backpack. He watched as the professor's eyes widened in anticipation.

"Professor," Kyle began, "I'm curious. What exactly do you think I found when I was exploring in the cave?"

The professor looked stunned, as if he thought Kyle should already know the answer to that question. He looked at Kaitlin as if he were hoping for her to come to his rescue. Kaitlin sat silently and waited for him to answer Kyle's question. "Well," the professor began, "I am not one hundred percent certain, but I think you may have found a very old tooth."

"And what makes you think that is what I found?" Kyle asked.

Again, the professor had a surprised look on his face. He sat there, not saying a word. He only looked at Kyle and Kaitlin as if they should already know the answer to their question. When the professor finally realized that Kyle truly did not know the answer, he responded, "You remember I told you about that archaeologist friend of mine? While we were in the cave, I had started to explain to you that there was a traditional story that had passed down from generation to generation? Well, that is how I know about the tooth."

Kaitlin jumped in and said, "Professor, you never finished telling us about the legend because Anthony showed up at the cave. If you tell us the story that your friend told you, then Kyle here will show you the tooth."

The professor sized Kaitlin up with his eyes and said, "You are very persuasive, Miss Kaitlin. Ja, indeed, I will tell you about the legend."

The professor sat quietly for a few moments, with a faraway look in his eyes. It seemed to Kaitlin that he was trying to remember the details of the story. It occurred to her that he may also be having difficulty knowing how to translate the legend into English so that they could understand. "According to my friend, the legend has been passed down that there were extra-large people that used to live on the Earth."

Kaitlin giggled, and Kyle couldn't help but join in with her. The professor looked very confused that they were laughing after this astounding revelation. In the midst of her laughter, Kaitlin looked at Kyle and said, "I think he means giants."

Kyle finally caught his breath and decided it would be best to explain to the professor why they were laughing. The blunder had been innocent enough, but Kyle wanted to correct the professor so he didn't go around saying the wrong thing to the wrong people.

"Professor, I apologize for laughing, but the expression that you used, 'extra-large people,' is often used in reference to people who are severely overweight. I believe that what you were referring to were people that were extra tall and had very large bone structures."

As the professor realized his mistake, he sighed heavily and said, "*Ja*, thank you, young Kyle. I would not want to cause people to feel bad. What was the expression that you used?"

"Giants," Kaitlin repeated.

The professor repeated the word to himself several times as if he were trying to memorize it. At last, he nodded his head and continued with his story.

"My friend told me that these giants, as you say, lived on the Earth thousands of years ago. They were not only quite different in size, but it seems that they also had the ability to understand things intuitively that people today take many hundreds of years to learn. Apparently, some archaeologists have discovered tools and machinery that appear to be ancient, but the technology is advanced far beyond what even we are capable of now. There have been findings of structures that have been built that seem impossible to have been made by a group of men that are the size we are familiar with today. Even the strongest men in this age would not have the ability to put these large stones into place."

"Hold on, Professor," Kaitlin interrupted. "If there really were giants, then where did they come from? And why don't we see them anymore?"

"Well, Miss Kaitlin," the professor answered, "I am not certain of where they came from. However, I do have a feeling about this, if you will kindly allow me to explain."

"Yes," Kyle answered for both of them, "please do."

"All right then," the professor continued. "Do either of you children read the Word of God?"

They both nodded their heads and Kaitlin answered, "Yes, we've read the Bible."

"Indeed, that is good to hear," said the professor. He continued, "In the Word, in what you call the Old Testament, there is a story about angels that came to Earth and intermingled with the women. The women bore children to the angels and those children were called 'Nephilim.' These Nephilim are those who many now believe were responsible for the advanced technology and the building of the structures with overgrown stones."

Kaitlin did not correct the professor this time, but she and Kyle both knew that he meant "oversized."

Kaitlin, who was always the curious one, was perplexed about how the remains of the giants had turned up in this area. "Professor," she asked, "isn't it true that the giants were typically found in the Middle East?"

"*Ja*," the professor said, nodding his head. "That is where many of their remains have been found."

"Well, then how did a large tooth come to be found in our area?" Kyle asked.

"Interesting question, young Kyle," the professor responded. "I have been told that there are two possible reasons for this. Some people believe that at one time all of the continents were joined together. This would explain why there are some remains found in various parts of the world. However, others believe that the giants traveled across the sea to other continents and then made those areas their home."

"How do you believe they got here, Professor?" Kyle asked.

The professor carefully pondered his answer and then he finally responded, "To be honest, I am not sure what I believe. I can see potential logic in both ways of thinking, but I have not come to a conclusion myself. I would be misunderstanding you if I said I knew which is right."

Kyle and Kaitlin both realized that the professor meant to say "misleading" instead of "misunderstanding," but neither corrected him.

The professor ended by saying, "I am hoping to be able to find more answers by studying whatever is found in that cave."

It seemed to Kyle that the professor had finished telling them about the legend, so he concluded that now might be a good time to show him the tooth. He decided that he would not say anything about the key, even if the professor appeared to be digging for more information. Kyle opened the lid and began to rummage through the tissues in the chest. With a flourish, he produced the little bag that held the tooth.

The professor reached out his hand as if he wanted to take it from Kyle. When he saw the look on Kyle's face, he asked politely, "May I?" Kyle nodded and hesitantly handed it over to the professor. The older man gingerly opened the bag and dumped the contents out into his hand. He examined the tooth carefully, turning it this way and that way. He held the tooth up so that the sunlight was shining on it. Then he slapped his knee with his free hand and exclaimed, "This is it, young Kyle! Now I will be able to do my studies and find out the answers to questions I have had for a very long time!"

Kyle did not want to dampen the excitement of the professor, but he was very reluctant to hand the tooth over to him. "If I agree to let you have the tooth," Kyle began, "will I ever get it back?"

"Yeah," Kaitlin agreed. "I know you have to run tests on the tooth, but Kyle *is* the one who found it. He should be able to keep it."

The professor looked perplexed, as if the thought of Kyle keeping such a find was beyond comprehension. He held the tooth up for all of them to see, and he sighed. "I do understand your wish to keep this for yourself, Kyle," he said. Then he continued, "If I had been the one to find it, I would feel the same way. But please understand that this one tooth will provide so many answers to questions that people have had for many, many years."

Kyle sat in silence, and Kaitlin wondered if the shock of the professor's request had left him speechless. Kaitlin knew that when Kyle had first agreed to show the tooth to the professor, he had not thought that he would be giving it up forever. Kaitlin knew her friend would do "the right thing," whatever he decided that might be.

After careful consideration, Kyle finally agreed. He was able to see that there would be a much greater benefit for all people if he allowed the professor to do his research on the tooth. Even with this knowledge, Kyle could not help but to feel a little sad at the loss.

This feeling of loss was similar to what he had felt when he knew he had to give up his Saturdays with his dad. He knew that what his dad was doing was for the good of the family, but he also knew that he would terribly miss their adventures to the beach.

"OK, Professor, you can keep the tooth," Kyle finally said, and then he let out a sigh.

The professor grew animated and bounded from his seat at the picnic table. "Ah, thank you so much, young Kyle!" he exclaimed. "You will be rewarded some day for giving up your treasure."

Kyle wasn't sure what to think about that, but regardless, he knew that he was doing the right thing.

"Besides, Kyle," the professor said and winked, "if you found the tooth in that cave, I'm sure you will find much more."

CHAPTER 16

That night Kyle was not able to sleep. The professor's words kept repeating over and over in his head. He began to imagine all of the possibilities of what he might find. *The funny thing is,* he thought, *I haven't really found anything else since I found the tooth and the key. I've explored so many of the rooms, I don't know how there can possibly be many more to go through.* Kyle finally began to drift off to sleep with images of the various rooms in the cave in his mind.

He was on the verge of being in a full, deep sleep when he envisioned a tunnel that he had seen on the other side of what he and Kaitlin now called the "Star Room." In reality, he hadn't really "seen" the tunnel when they were in the room. He hadn't been looking for another doorway. The truth was that it was something he must have seen in his peripheral vision while he and Kaitlin were talking with the professor.

He recalled that when he had first walked into the room, all he had been focused on were the Arachnocampa luminosa and trying to figure out what it was that was making the walls glow. Then, suddenly, Kaitlin had been there. He had no sooner gotten over his surprise at her appearance than the professor had revealed himself.

He hadn't really had time to process his surroundings. But now, when he was in a quiet room with no distractions, he could very clearly recall the tunnel at the end of the room opposite where he had come in. Kyle had the distinct impression that if he were to follow that tunnel it would lead him to a whole section of the cave that he had not known existed. He also felt very strongly that it would be in those rooms that he would make his greatest discoveries yet.

He and Kaitlin had planned to meet at the cave after school the next day. Right now, he felt so excited to tell her about his revelation that he was sure he would not sleep at all. As it turned out, Kyle was right about not being able to sleep. He tossed and turned all night, anxious for morning to come so he could tell Kaitlin about the tunnel.

****

The next day was a beautiful, sunny day. Kyle felt elated that he was able to ride his bike to school and not be stuck riding the bus. *One day less for Allan to tease me about something*, he thought. The only downfall was that it appeared Kaitlin had already left for school. It occurred to Kyle that the previous night, before Kaitlin had gone into her house, she had mentioned that she needed to ride the bus in the morning. He recalled now that she had told him that she needed to get to school early to study before a test in her English class. Although he understood that Kaitlin had no choice but to get to school early (which meant that she had to ride the bus to school), Kyle realized that now he would not be able to fill her in about the tunnel before he met her at the cave this afternoon. He felt a bit of disappointment creep over him. He had hoped that he could speak with her this morning and have her just meet him in the Star Room. Now it seemed that he would have to waste precious time searching for her in the cave. Not that her being there was a bad thing, but whatever time they would have to explore the new areas would be diminished by the two of them having to find each other.

Kyle groaned, and he wondered if the two of them would ever have any real exploration time in the cave. It seemed that somehow there was always an interruption. Kyle mulled over the fact that the appearance of the professor and Anthony had cut their explorations short. He also realized that having such a short amount of time between getting out of school and having to get home for dinner had also caused them to run out of time. He found himself wishing that the school year was over with so he and Kaitlin could have unlimited time to explore.

Well, at least not as *limited,* he thought to himself. There were only two weeks left in the school year. With that realization in mind, Kyle felt encouraged. After all, he was sure that the next two weeks would go quickly and that he and Kaitlin would have the entire summer to explore the cave.

He could feel the warm air on his face as he rode past the beach. Before he knew it, he was pulling into the parking lot of the school. As usual, he had been so lost in thought that the ride to school seemed like nothing but a blur. If he didn't know any better, he would have sworn that the bike had pedaled itself there.

Kyle guided the bike deftly to the bike rack and looked for any sign of Kaitlin. No luck. He was just finishing locking up his bike when he heard a female voice say, "Good morning, Kyle."

He looked up to see Kaitlin's friend Renee standing by her bike. "Hello, Renee," Kyle replied.

"Would you like to walk with me to class?" Renee asked.

"Sure," Kyle said.

They walked on toward the front doors of the school, talking about the Science Fair project that each was working on. Renee asked him what he was planning to do for his project. Kyle was about to reply that he had no idea and that he hadn't even started on it yet, when the image of the glowing worms popped into his mind. *Hmm . . .* he thought, *maybe I could get one of those little guys off of the cave walls and bring that in to school.* The idea had merit.

Thinking of the Star Room made Kyle think of meeting Kaitlin there later this afternoon. *It's too bad that I won't see her during the day to tell her where to meet me,* Kyle thought. Then, as if one of the Arachnocampa had lit itself up inside Kyle's head, a brilliant plan emerged.

"Hey, Renee," Kyle began, "you'll see Kaitlin in your social studies class later, right?"

"Yep, I will," she replied.

"Oh good!" Kyle almost shouted in relief. "Would you give her a message for me?"

"Absolutely!" Renee agreed, with a smile.

"Thank you, Renee," Kyle said. "You don't know how much I appreciate it. I would have texted Kaitlin, but, apparently, her mom and dad don't want her to bring her phone to school. They told her that she would be too distracted with the phone to pay attention in class. The funny thing is, I am pretty sure that they are right about that."

"My parents say the same thing to me," Renee answered. Then she followed with the question, "What would you like me to tell her, Kyle?"

Kyle thought for a moment and then finally said, "Tell her to meet me under the stars."

****

After school was over, Kyle hurriedly rode his bike to the beach. By the time he arrived, he saw that Kaitlin's bike was already parked at the rack. He quickly grabbed his backpack and ran to the path that led to the back entrance of the cave. As he reached the now familiar hole in the rock wall, he had his flashlight out, ready to fire it up. Kyle crawled his way through the first tunnel and made his way back to the Star Room. He was forced to switch off his flashlight and was temporarily blinded. In the past, he would have been afraid to call out for Kaitlin. However, now that they had met the professor face to face, he was no longer worried.

"Kaitlin, are you in here?" Kyle half asked, half shouted.

"Yep, I'm here," he heard her respond. She quickly flicked on her flashlight so that Kyle could tell where she was standing. Kyle slowly made his way over to her. When he reached the spot where she stood he said, "I see that you got my message from Renee."

"What message?" Kaitlin asked, with mock surprise in her voice.

Kyle was startled by her answer and said, "The message I gave her this morning to give to you in social studies."

"You mean the one about *meeting you under the stars*?" Kaitlin said in a sappy, sing-song voice.

Kyle knew that if he could see her face, she would be wearing a big cheesy grin. "Fine, tease away," he said with feigned offense, "but you got the message loud and clear, didn't you?"

"Sure did!" Kaitlin said and slugged him on the arm.

"What was that for?" Kyle shouted, while trying to rub the pain away from his arm.

"Oh, I don't know," Kaitlin replied. "I guess I just wanted to make sure you hadn't fallen asleep under the stars."

"Not a chance!" Kyle replied. "We have too much to do today for me to even think about napping."

"Why did you want me to meet you in here anyway?" Kaitlin asked.

"I'm glad that came up," Kyle answered. He continued, "Last night when I was trying to fall asleep I kept thinking about what the professor had said. I kept picturing all of the rooms that I have already explored in the cave and I felt disappointed because I didn't think there was much left to discover. But then, just as I was about to fall asleep, I thought of the Star Room. I remembered seeing something out of the corner of my eye when we were in here with the professor. It was one of those things that you don't really know you've seen, but later you remember it anyway."

"Ah, I see," Kaitlin replied. "So, what was it that you remembered seeing?"

Kyle pointed in the direction opposite of where he had entered the room. "Do you see it?" he asked.

He saw Kaitlin lean her head in the direction of the tunnel. "No," Kaitlin started to say, and then just as quickly she said, "Oh, wait . . . There it is! Kyle, that's so cool! Are we going to go in there?"

"ABSOLUTELY!" Kyle shouted with glee.

"OK, then," Kaitlin answered. "What are we waiting for?"

The two of them went through the tunnel with their flashlights blazing. They followed the twists and turns until they came to a room that at first glance didn't seem to have anything special about it. Kyle shone his flashlight about the room and discovered that the room was fairly long. Kaitlin did the same, but she aimed her flashlight at the ceiling.

"Kyle, look up there!" she exclaimed.

Kyle followed the direction of her light and saw the light glinting off an object that appeared to be attached to the ceiling. "I think that's quartz," Kyle said.

"I think so too," Kaitlin replied. "I sure wish we had a ladder that we could reach that thing with."

"Yeah, me too," Kyle agreed. "Maybe if we keep going we'll find more of it. That's what happened with the Star Room. Before I actually came upon the room itself, I found myself in a tunnel that led to it. When I first stepped into it, I didn't see much of anything, but the farther I went in, I started to see our little glowing friends more and more. I have a feeling that if we search further in this room we will find more of that quartz."

Kaitlin didn't wait a second longer. She stepped forward, shining her flashlight at the walls as she went. Kyle followed closely behind her. As Kyle had predicted, the farther they went into the room, the more they found of the glittering rock.

"Wow!" Kaitlin exclaimed. This is beautiful!"

"I seem to remember you saying that about the Arachnocampa too," Kyle teased.

"Oh, hush!" Kaitlin exclaimed, frustrated at his dig, but smiling all the same. "They are amazing in their own way . . ." she said with a slight hesitation in her voice.

"But?" Kyle interjected.

"Well, you know very well I'm not a big fan of creepy-crawly things," Kaitlin said and gave a little shudder. "At least with this stuff, it's predictable." Then she finished by saying, "I know it's not going to bite me or fall on me."

Just as she said that, a chunk of the quartz loosened from the ceiling and knocked her on the top of the head. "YOUCH!" she hollered.

Kyle picked up the offending piece of rock and handed it to her. "Do you still think it's beautiful now?" he teased.

"Of course I do!" she responded, and slugged him on the arm.

"Hey!" Kyle shouted. "The rock hit you, not me!"

"I know," Kaitlin responded, "but somehow it made me feel better."

Kyle could only grumble and rubbed his arm.

The two continued forward and found a whole wall covered with the quartz. Kaitlin reached up to wiggle the rocks to see if they would come loose. Most of them were too embedded in the walls for her to remove, but she kept trying anyway. Every so often she would come across one that would wiggle loose, and she would stuff it into her backpack.

"You better be careful, Kaitlin," Kyle teased. "If you fill your backpack too full you won't be able to run if we get chased."

Kaitlin shrugged her shoulders and said, "We don't have to worry about that anymore, remember?"

"I know," Kyle responded, "I'm just kidding."

He smiled a smile that stretched from ear to ear. "You still have to watch out, though," he said with a warning sound in his voice.

"Why?" Kaitlin asked, but she was still focused on the quartz in front of her.

"Because," Kyle teased, "if you get your backpack too full you might get stuck in one of the tunnels."

CHAPTER 17

K aitlin had finally finished stuffing her backpack full of quartz. It was so full that she could not close the zipper all the way.

"Boy, am I glad I'm not the one carrying your backpack!" Kyle teased her.

"Um, Kyle, about that . . ." Kaitlin began. She watched Kyle's facial expression change as he realized she was about to ask him to do her a favor.

"What is it?" Kyle asked.

"What is what?" Kaitlin replied coyly.

"Ugh!" Kyle responded. "I know you're going to ask me to do you a favor. So, out with it!"

"Geesh, Kyle, you don't have to get so snippy!" Kaitlin said in a somewhat whiny voice. "It's just that this quartz is so beautiful, and I can't fit enough into my backpack . . ."

"So you want to put some in mine, too," Kyle finished for her. "How much of this stuff do you need anyway?" he asked. "And what are you going to do with all of it?"

"I'm not sure yet, but I think I may have an idea for a really cool science project," Kaitlin answered.

"I am so confused!" Kyle said, shaking his head. "I thought that you had already started a science project."

"I did," Kaitlin began, "but when I saw these pieces of quartz it gave me an even better idea."

"Oh, all right," Kyle relented. "How many more do you think you'll need?"

Kaitlin began examining some of the pieces on the wall. "If you follow me with your backpack open, I'll show you," she said with a wink. Over the next several minutes, Kaitlin gathered more and more of the chunks of quartz, until she was finally satisfied.

"That should about do it," Kaitlin said triumphantly, as she dusted off the palms of her hands.

Kyle peeked inside of his backpack and realized that it was nearly half full. "Hey!" he said, sounding a little startled. "I thought you were only going to take a *few* more!"

Kaitlin gave Kyle her best puppy-dog look and said, "You want me to do my very best on this project, don't you, Kyle?"

"Of course I do," Kyle answered. "I just didn't think it would involve me carrying a sack of rocks for you."

Kaitlin teased him, saying, "Would you rather carry mine? I think if a puny little girl can handle this one," and she held up her overstuffed backpack for him to see, "then you can certainly handle *that* one!"

184

"Oh, fine!" Kyle said with defeat in his voice. "I'll carry your pretty rocks for you."

"Thank you!" Kaitlin said, sounding elated. She was silent for a minute as she scanned the room. "So what do we do now, Kyle?" she asked. Should we leave and go home, or should we keep going?"

Kyle shone his flashlight around the room, straining to see if there were any other tunnels that would lead to another room. As he swept the flashlight across an area that they had not really explored yet, he saw what appeared to be a doorway to another tunnel.

"Well, we haven't gone that way yet," he said, pointing in that direction.

Kaitlin saw what he was looking at and answered, "I'm game. But what are we going to do with these backpacks? I don't want to lug this thing around unless I have to."

"I agree," Kyle said. "We can leave them here in this room."

"Are you *crazy*?" Kaitlin asked. "What if someone finds them? Then I'll have to start all over. Or worse yet, I won't be able to use my really cool idea for my science project."

"Oh, brother!" Kyle said with a sigh. "Your rocks will be just fine in here. I promise that no stranger is going to come lurking around just to steal them."

Kaitlin reluctantly dropped her backpack on the ground next to her feet.

"Are you ready?" Kyle asked her.

"Yes," Kaitlin said hesitantly. She looked around the room and found an outcropping of limestone. "Hold on, I'll be ready in a minute." She grabbed her backpack and Kyle's and dragged them over until they were quite hidden behind the rock. As she wiped sweat from her forehead, she said, "OK, now I feel like they're safe."

Kyle could only sigh. He realized that when Kaitlin got like this there was no chance of talking any sense into her.

Kyle began to lead the way to what he thought had been an entrance. He drew nearer to it and shone the flashlight directly on it. When he stood before it, he realized that it was some sort of pillar. However, this pillar was not vertical as he would have normally seen them. This particular pillar was angled from the ceiling to the floor at an approximate forty-five-degree angle. The formation seemed a bit peculiar to him just because of the way it had formed. But then he noticed something even more intriguing. The pillar was not made of limestone. He could tell this because as he shone the flashlight beam on it, the light reflected off of it in places. As he moved the beam around, he noticed there were some areas that were so clear the flashlight shone right through the pillar.

Kaitlin came up behind him just as he was beginning to figure out the mystery of the pillar. "What on Earth, Kyle?" she asked in an awed tone. "Is that whole thing made out of quartz?"

Kyle was not quick to answer, but when he did, he said, "Yeah, Kaitlin, I think it is."

The two stood in silence, mesmerized by the sight. Finally, Kaitlin broke the quiet. "Doggone it! I wish I had some colored bulbs for my flashlight! Imagine how cool that would look!"

Kyle only nodded in agreement. He was trying to figure out how the quartz that they had seen growing in chunks along the walls and ceilings had somehow grown into a pillar. "Boy, oh, boy, this place never gets dull!" he said.

"You're right," Kaitlin said, nodding her head. "Never in a million years did I think that I could find a grimy, slimy old cave so fascinating!"

"All right then, Queen of Quartz, let's get this show on the road," Kyle teased.

Kaitlin could tell that although he was teasing her, now he was on a mission. "OK," she answered. "Where do you think this goes anyway?"

"I'm not sure, to be honest," Kyle answered. "One thing I do know is that we're both going to have to watch our steps getting over this thing," he said pointing to the pillar.

He slowly slipped first his right foot over it and then followed through with his left. "That was a little awkward, Kaitlin," he said in warning. "Here, give me your hand and I'll help you over."

Kaitlin smiled and held out her hand for Kyle. No sooner had she brought her second leg over the structure than the beam of her flashlight struck another pillar. This one looked identical to the one they had just crossed over, except that it stretched out from ceiling to floor in the opposite direction, and it had a slightly larger diameter than the previous one.

Kyle was about to step over the second pillar, when something else caught his attention. He put his hand back to stop Kaitlin from moving forward.

"What did you do that for?" she asked.

"LOOK!" was all he could say, then he pointed in front of them with his other hand.

As Kaitlin pointed her flashlight in that direction, she saw what appeared to be almost a spiderweb of sorts. The pillars of quartz covered nearly the entire space of the room. There were pillars of varying lengths and widths. They were all so close together that there was little space between them in which to maneuver around. Kyle realized that accomplishing the task of crossing the room would be challenging to say the least.

Most of the pillars seemed to have "grown" at an angle, beginning at the ceiling and eventually descending to the floor. Others grew from one wall to the other. When they looked at the pillars from a distance, it appeared that although they were separate, they still seemed to be all woven together in a criss-cross pattern.

Kyle told Kaitlin, "We are going to have to move very carefully through this room. These pillars are so close together that if we are not very careful, we may end up getting hurt. There are some pillars that we are going to need to climb over, and there are some that we will need to crawl under." Kyle shone his flashlight through one of the pillars. It was amazing to him that some areas of the pillar were opaque, while others were nearly translucent. Kyle thought to himself, *If I was not seeing this with my own eyes, I wouldn't believe this was possible.*

Kaitlin was unusually quiet for what seemed to Kyle like forever. And then suddenly, she burst into an explosion of emotion. "Oh, my goodness!" Kaitlin said. "Kyle, we have to come back here with my star light from home."

"What star light?" Kyle asked.

"You know," Kaitlin answered, "the one that has a dome decorated with the shape of stars. It has different-colored bulbs in it, so that when the stars are projected onto the ceiling, the stars change colors. How cool would that be in this room?"

"Um, Kaitlin," Kyle responded, "I hate to burst your bubble, but I'm thinking that light is way too weak to be used in this room."

"Aw, nuts!" Kaitlin said, with obvious disappointment. "I'm sure you're right, but you get the idea. I'll have to figure something out . . ." With that, Kaitlin's imagination ran wild, and she stood unmoving.

"Kaitlin," Kyle said, tugging on her sleeve, "I know that genius is burning, but we really should keep going. We're running out of time for the day."

Kaitlin shook her head as if she were slowly coming back to the present. "You're right, Kyle. Sorry about that."

"No problem," he answered. "OK, here we go. Now, why don't you let me cross over these things first, and then I'll help you."

"Kyle Marshall," Kaitlin began in an admonishing tone, "I'm a big girl. I don't need you to help me. I'll be just fine." As she said that she turned too quickly and stumbled backward over the pillar that would have been just in front of her. She landed with a thud on her bottom, and she let out a loud "oof" that echoed through the room.

Kyle had to bite his lip to keep from laughing. What a comical sight that had been, he thought. However, he knew that if he even dared to tease her after an incident like that had just happened, she would be extremely angry with him. He decided that, right now, the smartest thing to do was to not say a word. He held out his hand to her, and this time she took it without complaining.

Kaitlin brushed the dirt off her bottom as best as she could and said, "I'll follow you."

Kyle thought that it was a good thing the room was dark because then she couldn't see the enormous grin that had broken out across his face. He led the way, crossing first one pillar, and then turning around to help Kaitlin. When they first began crossing the pillars, Kyle had started to count them. After repeating the process of crossing, helping Kaitlin cross, and then stepping over the next one, the numbers got all jumbled together. *It doesn't matter anyway*, he thought.

Kyle noticed that they were getting closer to the other end of the room. "It's about time!" he said aloud.

Kaitlin, who hadn't spoken since she had taken the spill on the pillar, said vehemently, "You can say that again!"

Kyle had a flashback of when that phrase had caught the professor off guard and he had repeated what he had said, word for word. "It's about time," Kyle repeated, with a smile.

"Very funny, Professor," Kaitlin responded. She tapped him on the shoulder and said, "Last one there has to eat a worm!"

Kyle's mouth fell open, and the only thing he could utter was, "A WORM?"

Kaitlin, who saw that she had sufficiently startled him, took off running and leaping over the pillars as if she was a trained athlete participating in the Olympics. "Yeah, a WORM!" Kaitlin shouted with glee as she hurdled the last pillar. "Hey, Kyle, which would you like? A long, skinny one, or a short, fat one?"

"YECH!" Kyle said with a shudder. "I don't care if you won or not! I am not eating a slimy worm!"

Kaitlin laughed hysterically at the look of disgust and horror on Kyle's face. The sound of her laughter echoed through the room, and in spite of himself, Kyle couldn't help but smile. He finally caught up to Kaitlin and pointed his flashlight toward the opening that now loomed in front of them. He could only imagine what mysteries the room ahead might hold.

CHAPTER 18

The new room seemed vastly empty compared to the one they had just come from. Although many of the rooms he and Kaitlin had explored had been the same as this one appeared to be, Kyle still felt a slight sense of disappointment. After the literal obstacles that he and Kaitlin had just had to overcome, what he saw (or didn't see) ahead seemed like a letdown.

Kaitlin, who was all fired up after her victorious sprint to the end of the pillar room, was not so easily dissuaded. She shone her flashlight to and fro in the room, looking for any distinguishing item that might make it exploration worthy. Kyle did the same, but initially all he could see were bare walls and a floor that was almost completely covered by sand. It seemed that the wind had mysteriously been able to blow the sand from the beach outside into this very room.

"This is a little strange," Kaitlin commented. "I wonder how all the sand got in here."

"I was wondering the same thing," Kyle agreed. As he contemplated the sand that lay beneath his feet, he continued to shine his flashlight around the cave walls. The room was not large by comparison to what they had previously explored, but the walls jutted out at varying angles. It almost appeared that the walls formed some kind of zigzag pattern. Kyle realized that many of the walls were not visible from his and Kaitlin's current perspective.

Kyle noticed that the room seemed a little brighter than most of the ones they had been in. The only exception was the room with the Arachnocampa. He thought to himself, *We might not need our flashlights if there was even a little more light in this room.* Kaitlin seemed to be oblivious to this fact and was humming merrily as she worked her way toward the first outcropping of limestone. Kyle continued to stare at the ceiling and realized that this was the tallest ceiling they had encountered thus far. At the very tip-top it came to a point, almost as if it were the top of a pyramid. In the center of the highest point, Kyle observed that there was a hole which seemed to be about a foot in diameter. *That must be what is letting more of the light in,* Kyle thought. *I'll have to look around outside sometime to figure out where the top of this room is.*

He realized that now was not the time to be worrying about what the outside of the cave looked like. He could save that for later. They needed to be using every second they could get for their explorations inside. They had encountered so many interruptions that had caused delays that he didn't want to waste any more time. With that thought in mind, he began to move forward as Kaitlin had done. In his peripheral vision, he had seen that Kaitlin had already checked out the first wall. Now she had moved on to the second one that had come into view.

Kyle decided that he would proceed to the third wall and examine that one. He glanced back at Kaitlin as he approached the third wall but did not sense any sort of intense excitement on her part. With that being the case, he focused on the wall at hand. As he shone his beam on the now visible wall, he noticed that there were what appeared to be some sort of etchings. At first glance, it did not seem to be anything more than random scratch marks. However, he did notice that all of the walls they had seen so far seemed different somehow. In order to confirm his suspicions, he ran his right hand along the wall while he held the flashlight in his left hand. As he had suspected, the texture of these walls was significantly smoother, more so even than the ones in the prior room. It was as if someone had intentionally gone to the trouble to accomplish this result.

Kyle's attention was drawn once again to the etchings on the wall in front of him. He was standing at the end of the wall that connected to the previous outcropping. He moved the light in a sweeping motion from his end to the end that jutted out into the room. As he did this, he noticed more of these etchings that were close together. On a hunch, he lowered the flashlight about six inches. This time he swung the beam from the left back to where he stood. He watched as he moved the light and noticed that there appeared to be some sort of pattern to these etchings. They were evenly spaced apart and also seemed to have some type of specific shape to them.

Although he did not recognize what language it was, it appeared to be some ancient form of hieroglyphics. He puzzled over what they could mean and decided that it would be best to snap a picture of them with his phone so he could do some research on the Internet later. Once more he shone his flashlight on the wall, only this time he went back and forth over the entire wall. He swept the light from side to side, back and forth, until he had finally reached where the wall met the floor. He noticed that although some of the characters were similar, most of them had their own distinct shapes. He also noted that the characters covered the wall from just below the ceiling to the floor. It occurred to him that someone must have taken great pains to inscribe this message on the wall.

Kyle was about to call out to Kaitlin to come see what he had found when he heard her shout, "KYLE! YOU ARE NOT GOING TO BELIEVE THIS! COME SEE!"

Although he felt a tad bit disappointed that he would have to wait to show her *his* discovery, he could sense that she felt that what she had found was extremely important. He lowered the beam of his flashlight so he could see well enough to make it to the place where Kaitlin stood. When he arrived, he found her standing, staring and slack-jawed. Kyle asked her, "What is all the excitement about?" but got no response.

It was as if she had become temporarily mute because all she could do was point at the wall in front of her. Intuitively, he realized that the only way he would find out what had her in such a tizzy was to look for himself. His beam caught what appeared to be the drawing of a human foot. His eyes followed the beam and saw that the foot was attached to a leg, and the leg was attached to a torso. It seemed that what he was looking at was a picture of an extremely large human being.

"Wow!" Kyle exclaimed. "This is amazing! Whoever drew that picture made it pretty life-like!"

Kaitlin shook her head no. "That's not the half of it, Kyle!" she said in a breathless voice. "Look at the area where the arms are again."

"I saw them," Kyle assured her.

Um, no, you obviously didn't," Kaitlin said emphatically. "What you need to do is look on either side of the arms."

Kyle looked once again at the drawing of the arms, only this time he shone his flashlight just outside of the drawing of the man's left arm. He noticed that there appeared to be something resembling feathers near the man's arm. He swept the beam up to the height of the man's shoulder and noticed that the feathers cascaded from just above the top of the shoulder down to approximately his waist level. The feathers fanned out about three feet from the man's side. They appeared to be rounded above the shoulder and made a gradual sloping curve until they reached the man's waist. Near the waist, the feathers had somewhat of a tapered and asymmetrical look to them.

Kyle quickly shifted his flashlight to the man's right arm and saw that the other side was identical to the first one. Now it was Kyle's turn to be slack-jawed.

Kaitlin interrupted his thoughts with the question, "Kyle, do you think that this is a picture of an angel?"

Kyle nodded his head but couldn't really form the answer with his lips. After a few moments he was finally able to say, "This is so strange. Now it makes me wonder if what I found ties in with this picture."

"What did *you* find, Kyle?" Kaitlin asked with a hint of desperation in her voice. It seemed to Kyle that the more mysteries this cave revealed to Kaitlin, the more her passion grew for finding answers to those mysteries.

"Well, if you walk back with me to this wall," and here he pointed his flashlight at the one he had just been at, "I'll gladly show you. I really do believe that the drawing you found and what I found are tied together somehow."

"It wouldn't surprise me in the least," Kaitlin replied.

She followed Kyle to the outcropping and watched as he skimmed the flashlight over the hieroglyphics. "Do you have any idea what it says?" Kaitlin asked.

"No, unfortunately, I don't," Kyle replied. "I'm sure it's some kind of ancient language, but I will have to do some research on it in order to find out what it says."

"What, do you think you can learn an ancient language in a couple of hours?" Kaitlin teased.

"Of course not!" Kyle fumed. "But I think I can at least get an idea of what it says."

"Well, OK, then," Kaitlin said. "I hope you *can* figure it out because it's going to drive me crazy until you do!"

The two of them walked back toward the wall where Kaitlin had found the drawing of the angel. Kyle whipped his phone out of his back pocket and snapped a picture of it. "If I research the drawing and the hieroglyphs together, I may be able to figure out what they mean," he mumbled.

Kaitlin noticed that they were nearing the end of the room. "Boy, am I glad we stuck around long enough to see this place!" she exclaimed.

"I am too," Kyle replied. "I just wish we didn't have to leave soon."

"Kyle, school is almost over, and we will have all day long to explore this cave," Kaitlin said in a reassuring manner. She finished by saying, "I suppose we better head back now."

Kyle looked at her, and with disbelief in his voice said, "But Kaitlin, we haven't even finished checking out this room."

"I realize that," she answered. "I guess I was just thinking that after what we just found, nothing else would seem all that exciting."

"Are you *crazy*?" Kyle asked. "Who knows what else we could be missing if we don't keep going!"

"I suppose you're right," Kaitlin said with a sigh. "I was just kind of looking forward to getting my quartz home."

"Oh, for Pete's sake!" Kyle exclaimed. "Your rocks will be there when we finish exploring. Now, are you with me, or would you rather go home?" Kyle couldn't figure out why Kaitlin had seemed to lose her enthusiasm so suddenly.

Kaitlin only shrugged and answered, "I'm with you."

Kyle took off like a shot toward the last outcropping of wall, and Kaitlin went straight to the back of the room. Kyle decided it was probably best if he didn't try to prolong the search, so with a swift motion he passed the beam of his flashlight back and forth across the wall. It seemed to have the same smooth texture that the rest of the walls had, but Kyle could not find a trace of a hieroglyphic or a drawing. To him it seemed that whoever had designed this room had intended to use this wall as they had the others but had never quite gotten around to it. He was feeling somewhat disappointed and began to think that maybe he should have just listened to Kaitlin. Instead, he gave himself a pep talk and decided to at least search along the last stretch of wall between himself and where Kaitlin now stood. He followed the wall around the point where it jutted out and then curved around to meet the very back wall of the room.

Kyle was losing hope that they might discover anything else because the rest of the wall seemed to be as void of drawing or text as the last outcropping had been. However, as he moved further to his left, he noticed something that caught his attention. Apparently, Kaitlin had noticed it at the same time he had. She had walked up until she was standing right beside him.

"What is *this*?" she asked.

"It looks like a painting," Kyle responded.

As they surveyed the image before them, Kyle noted that there were several hands depicted. Some of them were lighter and some of them were darker. A few of the darker hands had a circle of a lighter color behind them, and the lighter hands had a circle of darker color behind them.

"It looks like they are all reaching for something," Kaitlin mused, as she took note of the outstretched palms and fingers.

"That is how it looks to me, too," Kyle agreed. "Except for this one," he said, and pointed his flashlight at a hand at the very bottom of the painting. "It looks like it's pointing at something, but it's pointing down instead of up."

"That seems very peculiar," Kaitlin said. "Hey, Kyle," she began, "do you think that the painting is trying to tell us something?"

Kyle was still staring at the hand with the finger pointing down. It was difficult to explain, but he had a feeling that the finger was pointing at *something*.

"Yeah, Kaitlin," he said, sounding distracted. "If I had to guess, I would think it means that the people the hands belong to are searching for something that is out of their grasp or beyond their reasoning."

"Hmm…" Kaitlin said, deep in thought. "I bet you're right."

Kyle, who was distracted by the painting, then stepped just slightly to his right, and he stubbed his toe on a pile of rocks. "Ouch!" he hollered.

"What happened?" asked Kaitlin. "Are you OK?"

Kyle, who was now seated on a rock and massaging his foot, answered, "My toe is throbbing terribly. If I could actually see it, I bet it would look the toes and fingers of the cartoon characters that are all red and blown up like a balloon."

Kaitlin could tell that Kyle was focused on his toe and that he didn't seem interested in capturing this particular artwork, so she decided to use her phone to take a snapshot of the painting. She began snapping pictures, one after another, until she was satisfied that she had sufficiently captured the painting. In the meantime, Kyle had gotten down on all fours and was starting to pick through the pile of rocks. He very carefully removed one after the other from the top of the pile. When he had progressed through a few inches, he stopped suddenly. Then with quiet fervor, he began to peel rocks away from the sides, a little at a time, as he had with the top.

Kaitlin, who had turned her attention on Kyle, noticed that he was intently digging in the pile of rocks. As she watched him, he appeared to her to be like a dog on the trail of a rabbit. Kaitlin watched with curiosity as he shuffled the rocks out of the way. "Do you see something?" she asked Kyle.

Kyle kept moving rocks, but said, "Yes, I think I do. Before you ask me what it is, I don't know for certain. I think I know, but I won't know if I'm right until I get these rocks moved."

"Can I help?" Kaitlin asked. "Sure, if you would like to," Kyle answered, "but you will have to be extra careful. This thing may be a little fragile."

Kaitlin knelt down next to Kyle and began to follow his lead with removing the rocks. Before she had moved more than a dozen, Kyle shouted with glee, "I've got it!"

"What? What is it?" Kaitlin asked.

"Are you sure you want to know?" Kyle teased. "Last time I showed you something like this you almost passed out!"

"I *did not* almost pass out!" Kaitlin retorted. After a beat, she asked, "Is it another body part?" She had asked the question jokingly, but when she saw Kyle's face, she knew she had hit the nail on the head.

"Yep!" Kyle said, and beamed. "It's a finger bone." He paused and then added, "The strange thing is that this is three times the size of one of my dad's fingers." Kaitlin made a face and started to open her mouth, but Kyle cut her off, saying, "I know. Eww, gross!"

Kaitlin smiled in spite of herself, but said in response, "Well, it is, you know."

"I know," Kyle answered, "but it's still really cool! I have a feeling that the professor is going to want to see this."

A figure appeared from out of the shadows. They could not see who it was, but they were startled to hear a male voice say, "He certainly will!" With that, Anthony lunged toward Kyle and grabbed the finger bone right out of his hand.

"What do you think you're doing, you big dummy?" Kaitlin shrieked.

Anthony, however, was not waiting around to answer. He darted toward an opening in the back wall of the cave that neither Kyle nor Kaitlin had noticed before now.

Kaitlin stood there staring, bewildered at what had just happened. Kyle, on the other hand, took off running after Anthony.

"Come on, Kaitlin!" he shouted. "We've got to get that finger back!"

CHAPTER 19

Anthony sped out ahead of Kyle and Kaitlin and was quite a distance ahead of them before Kyle's shock wore off. Kyle began to follow him, but Kaitlin seemed not to be in as much of a hurry as Kyle was.

"Kaitlin, come on!" Kyle shouted. "What are you waiting for?"

"Kyle, we have to get home soon, and our backpacks are still in the other room," she replied. "What if we aren't able to go back and get them?"

"Kaitlin," Kyle said, sounding exasperated, "you are my best friend, but sometimes you drive me nuts! The backpacks will still be there waiting when we come back tomorrow!"

"But Kyle," Kaitlin said, "I wanted to bring that quartz home to work on my science project."

"I understand, Kaitlin, truly," Kyle said in a soothing voice. And then with a greater urgency he said, "I promise that I will help you with your project as much as you want. Right now, we have to worry about finding Anthony and getting that finger back from him."

"What about our homework?" Kaitlin asked, on the verge of whining.

"I don't want to be late turning my homework in either, Kaitlin," Kyle responded. "I'm just not sure that we have much of a choice in this matter."

"All right . . . fine," Kaitlin answered. "Let's go find Anthony."

Kyle didn't have much hope of finding the thief by the time they had settled the matter of the backpacks. However, he decided that he at least had to try. He consoled himself with the knowledge that at least he knew where to find the finger bone if they couldn't catch up with Anthony. *Certainly,* he thought, *Anthony will hand it off to the professor. He will study the remains to see if they belong to the same person that the tooth belonged to.* He felt rather dismal that such a find had literally been ripped right out of his hands before he even had a chance to examine it. The tooth had been one thing. At least he had had the chance to look at it and ponder why it might have been there in that cave. *But this,* he thought, *is very different. He stole it right out of my hand!*

Kyle ran as fast as his legs would allow him. The tunnel that Anthony had escaped through was unfamiliar territory for Kyle. As a result, he had to use his flashlight at every turn. His chase of the thief seemed to take an eternity. He tried to make note of the direction the tunnel followed and which room he ended up in. As he entered one such room, he noted that there was the sound of water dripping and splashing into a pool of water below. *I'll have to check that out tomorrow,* he thought. As much as his curiosity was getting the better of him, he knew that there was no time to stop now. He wondered how Anthony was able to know the layout of the cave well enough to find him. To him, it seemed that the room was so obscure that no one could have possibly found it. *But Anthony did . . .* he reminded himself.

Kyle turned around a few times during his trip through the tunnels and the rooms to make sure Kaitlin was still with him. She had said nothing as they attempted to catch up to Anthony. Now he called out over his shoulder, "Kaitlin, are you there?"

"Yes," she answered, trying to catch her breath. "I'm here."

"Good!" Kyle said. "I think we are almost to the outside of the cave, and I don't see any sign of Anthony. I'm sure he's long gone by now. I guess we have to get home soon anyway."

Kaitlin looked at her watch and answered, "You bet your sweet petunias we do! It's nearly five o'clock!"

With that, Kyle doubled his speed until he finally reached the cave's exit. When he was able to look around and get his bearings, he realized that this entrance was not one that he had discovered on his own. He followed the path down toward the parking lot and was able to establish that this particular entrance to the cave was about midway between the bottom of the path and the one that he normally used on the backside of the beach wall.

Kaitlin emerged from the entrance at nearly the same time that Kyle was figuring out where he was. "Hey, Kaitlin," Kyle shouted to her, "did you notice that we came out in a different spot than we usually do?"

Kaitlin looked around her and shook her head. "I didn't notice that until you pointed it out," she responded. "I'm glad you figured it out," she continued, "because it will make getting back to our backpacks that much easier."

"Oh brother!" Kyle said and sighed. Then he asked her, "Do you see any sign of Anthony anywhere?"

Kaitlin craned her neck to look around her. She even took a few steps in the direction of the path that led to the beach before she answered him. "No, Kyle, I don't see him."

Kyle flopped down on the path, completely discouraged by this turn of events. He could only hope that they would somehow be able to meet up with the professor and have a talk with him. Kyle was sure that the professor would understand how important this find had been. He would also understand how frustrating it was to find something so valuable and have it stolen away only moments later.

Kyle stood up once again and motioned to Kaitlin. "Come on, Kaitlin," he said. "We better head home before we end up being hunted by our parents instead of Anthony! I'd rather be hunted by him than my mom!"

Kaitlin caught up with him on the path. "Kyle," she answered kiddingly, "I'd rather be hunted by anyone other than your mom!"

****

Later that evening, Kyle sat on his bed, sulking over the loss of the finger bone. He recalled the futile attempt to chase Anthony. He also remembered trying to hurry Kaitlin along so they could possibly catch him. He shook his head in wonder over the inconsistency of his friend. His mind traveled back to the scene in the room of pillars and Kaitlin exulting over her victory in reaching the end of the room before him. He could hear her teasing him about eating worms (which still made him shudder to think of). He could picture her being so excited about entering the next room to see what they would find next.

Kyle sighed deeply. *I do not understand her,* he thought, *not one little bit! But she is a girl after all . . .* His thoughts trailed off and he was in an almost dreamlike state, when he heard a tone come from his phone.

Kyle quickly grabbed it from his dresser. He thought it might be Kaitlin sending him a message. He imagined her apologizing for her behavior earlier that day. However, the phone number that he saw displayed was not a familiar one. He felt just a little wary about checking the message now. From as far back as he could remember, his mom had drilled into his head that he should never talk to strangers. As he got older, his mom had warned him that sometimes strangers were able to use other forms of communication, such as a phone or a computer. Kyle realized that, although this could be one of those situations, it was highly unlikely. So, in spite of the voice of his mom inside his head telling him to ignore it, he went ahead and opened up the text message anyway.

"Young Kyle," the message began. From the first two words, Kyle was able to deduce that the message was from the professor. "I hope you don't mind, but I found your phone number listed on your Facebook page, and I decided to try to contact you this way. You are a smart young man Kyle, but I hope that you will be smart enough to remove your phone number from Facebook. You never know who might try to contact you." Here, Kyle paused in his reading of the text message and smiled at the irony of the professor's words. Technically, the professor was a stranger and he was contacting Kyle the same way that he was warning Kyle about other strangers contacting him. Kyle determined in his mind that it probably would be a good idea to remove his phone number from the site, and he decided to do so after he read the professor's message. For now, Kyle continued to read the rest of the message. It continued, "I apologize for speaking to you this way. I do not mean to make you frightened." In his mind, Kyle could just hear his mom saying, "See, I told you so." Kyle shook his head to clear it and continued to read the professor's message. "I understand," it said, "that my very ignorant nephew took something of value from you this very afternoon. I can only ask you to forgive his actions. I speak with him and he says he will never do such a thing again. I have your finger"—here Kyle laughed at the image of the professor having his very own finger—"and I will keep it very safe! I study it as I study the tooth you gave to me. I think with all of my heart that we will have an amazing discovery from these two treasures."

Kyle shook his head in bewilderment. He realized that he could not fault the professor for the actions of his nephew. And, in truth, Kyle was glad that the professor was able to do research and tests on the tooth and the finger in order to determine where they came from. *If the professor is right,* Kyle thought, *this may be one of the greatest discoveries of all time. At the very least, it may lead people to an awareness of their Creator.* Kyle was painfully aware that there were many people who flat out denied that there was one greater that had created everything that we are aware of, and even everything that we aren't aware of. He was thankful that he and his parents and Kaitlin and her family had a firm grasp on their faith.

As he thought of Kaitlin, he realized that he should give her a little heads-up about the message from the professor. He reached for his phone once again and searched through his contacts until he found Kaitlin's name. He pushed the button to create a new text message and wrote the following message: "Kaitlin. Heard from the professor. He has the finger bone. Will tell you about it tomorrow. Meet you at the cave after school. We will go to the pillar room and get our backpacks first. Don't worry, your quartz is safe." After he finished the message, he placed his phone on the dresser next to his bed. Then he snuggled into his pillow and burrowed under his blankets until he drifted off into dreamland.

CHAPTER 20

After school the next day, Kyle did as he said and waited for Kaitlin in the pillar room. He was beginning to grow impatient as the minutes ticked by, and almost decided to set off on his own little expedition. Just as he was about to give up on waiting for Kaitlin, he heard a whistle in the distance. That, he recognized, was Kaitlin's signal that she was approaching.

Finally, she appeared in the room and asked, "So, tell me about the professor."

Kyle was a little bit on the frustrated side that she had taken so long to get here, but he shook the feeling off. He answered her, saying, "The professor is studying both the finger bone and the tooth. He apologized for Anthony stealing it from me like he did. He also assured me that it would never happen again."

"I wouldn't count on that!" Kaitlin exclaimed. Then she continued, "That Anthony seems to have a mind of his own."

"Maybe that's because he does," Kyle said in a snippy tone.

"Kyle," Kaitlin began, "you know what I mean! It seems that Anthony just does what he wants, even if the professor tells him to behave himself."

"Well, I have a feeling that this time it will be different," Kyle answered.

"If you say so," Kaitlin said, but she did not sound at all convinced. Kyle had no reply to her comment.

"So," Kaitlin said, trying to sound more light-hearted than she felt, "where are we off to explore today?" She grabbed her backpack with the load full of quartz.

Kyle reached behind the large limestone formation and grabbed his pack as well. As he leaned over he replied, "Do you remember when we chased Anthony yesterday?" Kaitlin nodded. "Well," Kyle continued, "There were two rooms that we went through that I absolutely must explore!"

"Do you remember anything about them?" Kaitlin asked.

"Hmm . . ." Kyle began, "to be honest, I really wasn't paying all that much attention to the first one. The one that stuck out to me was the second room that we went through. I heard the sound of water dripping."

"Big deal!" Kaitlin said. "I've heard that sound in at least a few of the rooms that we've been in so far."

"Yeah, I know," Kyle responded, "but this sound was different. The water wasn't dripping onto dry ground. It made a splashing sound, like it was falling into a pool."

"Well, then," Kaitlin said with a wink, "that may have some more possibilities."

The two of them continued through the pillar room and then into what they now called the "Drawing Room." Neither one of them stopped to take the time to reexamine anything they had found the day before. Their goal today was to find new and better discoveries. Kyle led the way through the tunnel that emptied out into the first room he had run through while chasing Anthony.

"Kyle," Kaitlin blurted out into the darkness, "did you get in trouble for not having your homework to turn in?"

Kyle mumbled something in response, but Kaitlin couldn't understand him. "What was that?" she asked.

"YES!" he said in a very grumpy voice. "I got in trouble in every class that I went to today!"

"I did too," Kaitlin answered. "I guess maybe you're used to it, but I'm not . . ."

"I am NOT used to it!" Kyle hollered. "I don't want to get in trouble any more than you do! I hate getting into trouble, and I hate to disappoint my teachers and my parents! I just didn't think things were going to work out the way they did yesterday."

"I didn't either," Kaitlin agreed. "Hey, maybe next time we can take our homework out of our backpacks and leave it by our bikes. That way, if we have to leave our packs behind, we won't lose our homework too."

Kyle thought about her plan, shrugged, and said, "I guess that's not such a bad idea."

Kaitlin slugged him in the arm. "It's a great idea, and you know it, Kyle!" she said emphatically.

Kyle said nothing in reply, but smiled at her, and then continued on into the room. He switched on his flashlight and swept it around the perimeter. In the background, he could see that there were large chambers carved out of the wall. The chambers seemed to cover the entire room. To Kyle, it appeared that they were almost a rectangular shape. However, they were slightly rounded at the corners, which gave them somewhat of a circular appearance.

Kaitlin shone her flashlight where Kyle had been pointing his and asked, "What do you suppose those were used for?"

"I'm not exactly sure," Kyle began, "but if I had to guess, I would say that they were some kind of living quarters."

Kaitlin shone her flashlight around at all of the chambers and then replied, "I'm not so sure about that. They seem awfully small for people to be living in. Can you imagine how small those people would have to be to actually live in a space like that?"

"Well, I could if they were kids like us," Kyle answered.

"Kyle Marshall, who are you kidding? Even I couldn't live in a space that small. And I'm puny!" she said for emphasis.

"I suppose you're right," Kyle said. Then he asked her, "So, what do you think they were used for then?"

Kaitlin stood still and quiet, pausing to think before she answered. "I have an idea, but I would like to check them out first."

"Sounds like a great plan to me!" Kyle responded.

With that, the two of them walked across the floor of the main part of the room until they came to a staircase. Kyle pointed the beam of his flashlight and tried to follow the direction that the stairs took. He was able to do so to a point, but then he realized that the stairs must have curved around, because he lost sight of them.

Kaitlin looked at Kyle and said, "I'll follow you."

"Chicken, bawk, bawk!" Kyle teased mercilessly.

"I AM NOT CHICKEN!" Kaitlin hollered, and as she did, she took off running up the stairs.

"Hey, wait for me!" a startled Kyle said.

****

Kaitlin entered the second tunnel with Kyle following closely behind her. The two had explored many of the chambers and found that there really wasn't much to be found in them. In all of the rooms, they had found the same structures carved out of the stone. At first, they both thought that they were some type of bed, and so they assumed that what Kyle had originally thought had to have been true. However, as they had discovered a bit later, the beds contained piles full of some type of ashes. In some of the rooms, they had found bits of clothing. In others they had found relics of jewelry.

Kaitlin had wanted to keep the jewelry, but Kyle had insisted that she leave the things where she found them. "It wouldn't be right," he had told her. "Those things belonged to someone."

Kaitlin had groaned because the pieces of jewelry were so unique. She told Kyle, "I would love to give one to Mom as a present. You could give one to your mom, too," Kaitlin had suggested, in an almost pleading voice.

But Kyle had said, "No way. Don't you get it, Kaitlin? These weren't *living* quarters! These chambers were where the people buried their dead."

As much as Kaitlin had wanted that jewelry, even she had to admit that it would be somewhat like stealing to take it. And so the two of them had moved on to the next room.

It was at the entrance of that very room that Kyle stopped Kaitlin in her tracks and whispered vehemently, "Shh . . . Kaitlin, do you hear it?"

Kaitlin paused long enough to listen to the sound emanating from the room before her. "I hear it, Kyle," she said. "I hear the drip, splash, drip, splash. How did you even notice that yesterday when we were chasing Anthony? I wasn't paying attention to anything except for trying to find him. Well, that and how much trouble I would be in if I got home late."

"I'm not really sure," Kyle answered. "I just heard it."

Kyle moved further into the room with his flashlight directed in front of him. As it turned out, it was a good thing he was shining the light ahead of him. Had he gone any further, he would have stepped directly into a pool of water. Kaitlin stepped forward to get a better look at the pool. The water around the edges of the pool seemed to have a murky appearance.

"If I had to guess," she told Kyle, "I would say that this is some type of bacteria. I just learned about this in Science class. There are some bacteria that can grow in dark areas of caves by using minerals as their source of energy."

"And I would have to guess that you are correct, Sherlock," Kyle said with a smile. Then he winked and continued, "It's funny, I just had that very same lesson in my Science class."

Kyle shone his flashlight toward the middle of the pool and noticed that the water was a crystal-clear blue color.

"That is probably the most beautiful pool of water I have ever seen," Kyle exulted. "You can see almost all the way to the bottom."

"It looks pretty deep," Kaitlin said. Then she posed some questions to Kyle. "How deep do you think it is? And where do you think the water is coming from?"

Kaitlin watched Kyle's face intently and saw that he was pondering her question. It took him a few minutes to respond, but then he finally answered, "Well, it seems to me that although the water is dripping from the ceiling, it would take an awfully long time for that pool to fill the way that it has. I'm not saying that it's impossible, but I have another theory for how all that water got in there."

"I'm waiting . . ." Kaitlin said when he paused.

"Well, as I was looking down into the center of the pool," Kyle explained, "I noticed that there seemed to be a hole at the bottom. It's hard to tell from here, but it looks as if it's about three feet wide. I also noticed that there were some bubbles coming up through the hole. Now, I'm just guessing, but to me those bubbles mean that the water is coming from somewhere other than the drips falling from the ceiling."

"OK. Then," Kaitlin asked, "where do you think the water is coming from?"

"You're not going to believe me," Kyle said, sounding hesitant to answer.

"Sure I will," Kaitlin reassured him. Then she followed the statement up with a teasing remark. "You may not be the smartest kid in school, but I still believe in you, Kyle."

"You're hilarious, Kaitlin!" Kyle said with a tone of mock disgust.

"All right, the suspense is killing me!" Kaitlin nearly shrieked. "Just tell me already."

"Are you sure that you want to hear?" Kyle asked.

"Of course I am, Yoda!" Kaitlin teased again.

Kyle grumbled at that remark but then finally answered, "I think that there is some sort of passage that leads from this pool to the ocean. I am guessing that the ocean is slowly seeping into that passage, and that the water, instead of going back out into the ocean, gets trapped in this pool."

Kaitlin was quiet for only a second before she answered, "That sounds like a reasonable explanation to me."

The two of them walked around the perimeter of the pool. Kyle interrupted the silence and said, "I see another tunnel over there, Kaitlin," and he pointed opposite of where they were standing.

"Well, how are we going to get over there?" Kaitlin asked.

"The only way we can," Kyle answered. "We'll have to swim. I know that you're not that great of a swimmer, Kaitlin, but I will—"

Kyle was interrupted by an excited shout from Kaitlin. "KYLE! Look at this! Oh, my goodness, it's . . ."

"Beautiful?" Kyle interjected, with a hint of sarcasm.

Kaitlin gave him a look that could have shot daggers at him, but answered, "Yes, it's beautiful! Come see for yourself."

Kyle ambled over to where Kaitlin stood and saw that she was holding some sort of gem. "It's an opal," Kaitlin explained. "Only I've never seen one like this before in my entire life!"

"Yeah," Kyle agreed, mocking her, "all twelve years of it!"

"Oh hush!" Kaitlin scolded. "When you take a look at this thing, you'll know that I'm telling the truth."

Sure enough, when Kyle examined the opal, he noticed that it had literally every color of the rainbow. Not only was the gem amazing because of the variety of colors, but it was even more remarkable because of the intensity of them. "It truly is beautiful," Kyle said with all sincerity.

"I know," Kaitlin said, with an air of sophistication. "I'm taking it home with me." She looked at Kyle to see if he would have anything to say about it.

"I won't argue with that," he assured her.

"Yippy!" Kaitlin screeched and threw her fist into the air triumphantly. "So, Kyle, what's on the agenda for tomorrow?"

"Tomorrow?" Kyle said. "Tomorrow we're going swimming!"

CHAPTER 21

The next morning Kyle realized that he should probably remind Kaitlin that she may need a swimsuit for their little expedition. *At the very least*, he thought, *she will need a T-shirt and some comfy shorts.* He already had his swim trunks stuffed into his backpack. He hoped he wasn't too late to catch her before she left for school. He pushed the icon to send text messages and scrolled down until he found Kaitlin's name. "Hey, Kaitlin," he typed, "just thought you might want to bring a suit for later today." He waited for a minute to see if she would respond.

He looked at the clock and realized that he needed to get out the door and head to school. The thought of having his first-hour teacher glare at him for being late did not sound all that appealing. Kyle began to make his way down the stairs, when suddenly he heard a "ding" indicating that he had received a message. He pulled his phone out of his pocket to look at the message and nearly took a tumble down the stairs in the process. He gripped the railing to steady himself and chuckled slightly. *Boy*, he thought, *who would have guessed that being at home could be more dangerous than being in that cave?* He opened the message from Kaitlin and read, "Kyle, you know I don't wear tuxes. I'm a *girl*! LOL. I'll bring it with me. See you this afternoon."

Kyle smiled at Kaitlin's silly little joke. The image of her in a tuxedo jumping into that pool in the cave made him laugh. Kyle slipped into the kitchen to grab some of the bacon that his mom had cooked for breakfast that morning. He didn't see his mom approaching, but he heard her ask, "What are you laughing about?"

"Oh, nothing really," Kyle replied. "Kaitlin just sent me a funny text message."

"I see," his mom said. "I thought maybe my hair looked extra frizzy today."

Kyle began to think that he was never going to live down the comments he had made the day his mom had offered to take him and Kaitlin to school. But then his mom gave him a wink, and he knew that all was well.

"Did you get enough bacon?" his mom asked. "Maybe you should bring a little extra for Kaitlin."

Kyle smiled at her suggestion. He and his mom had chuckled a few times over the memory of Kaitlin stuffing her mouth with sandwich after sandwich. Even his dad had gotten a good laugh out of the story. "I thought teenage boys were the ones that were supposed to eat like that!" he had said in an amused tone.

The thought of his dad made Kyle think about how much he wished his dad had been able to explore the cave with him. He shook the sad thought away just as quickly as it came. Then he reminded himself to be thankful that he was able to share the experience with Kaitlin.

Kyle glanced at the clock on the wall and noticed that he was a few minutes behind schedule. "Mom, I have to get going. I should have left already, but I started thinking about the joke Dad made about Kaitlin and the sandwiches. It made me a little sad. It seems like I hardly get to see him anymore."

"Oh, honey," his mom consoled him, "I understand. I miss having him around too."

Kyle's eyes began to well up, so he swiped at them. His mom looked as if she were going to hug him, but Kyle really didn't feel like being hugged. "Thanks, Mom," he said, "but I really need to get going. I love you."

His mom looked a little disappointed. However, she recognized that he needed his space to deal with his emotions. "I love you, too, Kyle," she responded.

Kyle charged out the door and headed for his bicycle.

****

Kaitlin was waiting in the Pool Room by the time Kyle got there that afternoon.

"Hey, Kaitlin," Kyle said in greeting. "Where's your suit?"

"Oh sure," Kaitlin teased, "no 'Did you have a good day, Kaitlin?' Or 'I'm so glad to see you.'"

Kyle realized he should be used to her sense of humor by now, but it took him a minute to realize that she was joking. In a smart-aleck voice he said, "I'm glad to see you, Kaitlin."

"Wow, I can just feel the excitement oozing out of you!" Kaitlin retorted. "What's wrong with you today?"

Kyle realized that he had been a little on the snippy side with her, so he answered, "I'm sorry. I've just been missing my dad. I've been a little bummed out all day."

"Oh," Kaitlin replied, "I get it. I'm sorry, Kyle. I know it's hard for you."

"Yeah," was all that Kyle was able to say back.

The two stood in silence briefly, and then Kaitlin suggested, "How about we do a little swimming?"

Kyle's face brightened, and he said, "That sounds good! But seriously, Kaitlin, where is your suit? I thought I told you that you would need it—"

"Relax, you big worry wart! I already have it on under my clothes. I put it on at school because I didn't think there were changing rooms anywhere around here," Kaitlin responded with a wink.

"Great! Then you're ready to go," Kyle said, with the most enthusiasm Kaitlin had heard from him so far.

"You bet your sweet cheeks I am!" Kaitlin replied.

Kyle gave her a funny look. She smiled a huge smile, and he knew she was just trying to get a rise out of him. He ignored her and pulled off his T-shirt.

"OK, Kaitlin, here's the scoop," Kyle began.

"Is it chocolate?" Kaitlin teased. "You know that's my favorite!"

"Sure," Kyle replied, "chocolate it is. So, last time we were here I was checking out the entrance to the tunnel over there. I already knew that we were going to have to swim to get there, but originally, I thought we might just be able to swim right through the doorway. The thing is, after I looked at it a little more closely, I could see that the rock extends down below the surface of the water. I think that means that we are going to have to dive down and swim under water for a bit before we make it into the other room."

"Oh . . ." was all Kaitlin said. Kyle could sense that she was feeling rather nervous about this unexpected turn of events.

"Listen, Kaitlin," he said in a measured and soothing voice, "I brought some goggles for us so that we can see where we are going. I will go first, and I will be looking out for anything that might seem dangerous. If there is any sign that we should turn back, I promise you, we will."

Kaitlin sighed deeply, squared her shoulders, and said in a determined voice, "OK. I'll do it. But what happens if I run into trouble somehow? How will you know?"

"Just tap me on my foot and I'll check on you," Kyle replied.

"That sounds reasonable," Kaitlin answered.

"Good," Kyle exclaimed, "then are you ready?"

"As ready as I'll ever be," Kaitlin said.

"Then let's go! One, two, three!" Kyle said with a shout.

And with that, they jumped into the pool.

****

Kyle dove down deeper into the water until he was able to see the entrance to the tunnel that led to the next room. He decided that before he entered the tunnel it would be wise to check on Kaitlin to see how she was doing. From what he could tell, she appeared to be doing well. He could see bubbles coming out of the snorkel that was attached to the mask. He felt that now it would be safe to enter the tunnel and that she would be able to follow him without any issues. Before he made a move to go forward he pointed first at Kaitlin and then at his feet. He watched as she nodded her head yes to confirm that she understood his meaning.

Kyle proceeded into the mouth of the tunnel and saw that the walls on the sides seemed to be fairly smooth. He could only guess that over time the water had eroded any sharp edges of the rock. This would make their journey all that much easier, because they would not have to worry about injuries from the rock or their suits getting snagged in various places. Kyle realized that although the tunnel was not extremely wide, they had plenty of room to swim through it. From his vantage point, he could see that the tunnel itself was not very long. That meant that they would reach the new room before long.

He felt bold now, knowing that he and Kaitlin could proceed safely to the end of the tunnel, so he swam a little faster than he had before. In a matter of seconds, Kyle had reached the entrance to the next room. He broke the surface of the water and was able to pull himself up on the rock ledge that became the floor of the room. Kaitlin swam up right behind him and hoisted herself onto the ledge as well. The two of them sat for a minute, catching their breath, before either of them spoke.

"Well, that wasn't so bad," Kaitlin said. "I just noticed that you have that key on a string around your neck, Kyle."

"Yeah," Kyle replied. "I'm not sure why, but I had a feeling that we would need to have it with us. I have been looking in all of the other rooms for something, anything, that the key would work in, but I was never able to find anything. I know that we have explored nearly all of the cave now, so it just seemed logical that this would be the place that it was used in."

"I can understand that," Kaitlin responded.

"Are you ready to go check this place out?" Kyle asked.

"Absolutely!" Kaitlin agreed.

The two of them stood up and spun around to get a good view of the room before them. The room itself was not all that wide, but they noticed that the ceiling of the cave was extremely high compared to those of the previous rooms. The walls appeared to be made of the same limestone that they had seen everywhere else. For all intents and purposes, besides the high ceiling, there did not appear to be anything significant or unusual about this particular room.

Kyle felt almost disappointed because he had been sure that this would be the one room where they would find their biggest discovery. He had to remind himself that appearances could be deceiving. With this in mind, he began to walk the perimeter of the room, searching for any clues to how the key might be used. Kaitlin had gone to the opposite side of the room and was doing the same thing.

Kyle walked slowly, examining every inch of the wall in front of him, from the floor to the ceiling. As he continued to move forward, he grew more and more discouraged when he saw that nothing looked out of place. However, because he was not one to give up easily, and he had such a strong feeling that he would find something of great importance here, he continued to move forward, always searching with his eyes. He ran his hands along the wall in order to determine if there were any irregularities that would indicate some kind of opening. He had made his way to the back wall of the cave when he hit pay dirt. There was a gap in the wall approximately two inches wide. As he looked up he saw that the gap continued all the way up the wall until it nearly reached the ceiling. Kyle's eyes followed the gap back down all the way to the floor. He realized that this could be nothing more than a crack in the wall, but something told him that this was not the case.

Kaitlin had made her way around the wall and stood about twenty feet opposite from Kyle. "Hey, Kyle," she shouted out excitedly. "I think I've found something."

"I may have, too," Kyle said. "What do you see?" he asked her.

"Well, there's a crack here that's pretty wide. It seems to run from the floor to the ceiling, or at least almost to the ceiling."

"That's interesting," Kyle began. "I found the same thing over here. I wonder . . ." And here he trailed off. He moved slightly to his left and began examining the wall for some place that the key would fit. There seemed to be nothing at eye level, so he searched the wall straight above where he had been looking. Approximately five feet above where he now stood, he saw what appeared to be several holes in the wall. He could tell that there was a distinct shape to the holes, but it was difficult to determine whether the key would fit in them.

"Kaitlin, my dear friend," he said in a syrupy-sweet voice, "I need you to help me with something."

"Sure, Kyle," she answered. "What do you need me to do?"

Kyle wasn't looking forward to explaining his thoughts to her because he was certain that she would want no part of it. He realized, though, that there was only one way that his plan would work, so he plunged ahead. "Well, I think I can see where the key fits into the wall. The problem is that it's up much too high for me to reach on my own . . ." he said with a little bit of trepidation.

Kaitlin, who was a perceptive girl, finished his thought. "So, you need me to climb up on your shoulders to see if the key fits in those holes." Surprisingly, she didn't seem appalled at the idea. She confounded Kyle when she said, "Let's do this! I think that we've found some type of door, and I want to see if this key works to open it."

Kyle sighed with relief and motioned for her to come over to where he stood. When she moved close to him, he squatted down enough for her to climb up onto his shoulders. Kaitlin grabbed both of his hands with hers and held on tight. Once he was sure she was ready, Kyle moved himself to a full standing position and raised her up to the level of the holes.

"Kyle," he heard her say as she looked down at him, "it looks like you may be right. I think the key *will* fit here. The problem is, I'm not close enough to try it. Well, that and the fact that you are still wearing the key around your neck."

She giggled slightly when Kyle answered sheepishly, "Oh, yeah, I guess that might help."

"It might," Kaitlin agreed.

Kyle slowly lowered Kaitlin to the ground. He removed the key from around his neck and handed it to her.

"Why don't you wear it around your neck until you are close enough to use it," Kyle suggested. "I'm afraid that if you try to hold onto it while I'm lifting you up there, you may drop it. Then we would have to go through this a third time," he finished, pointing at his shoulders.

"It's not so bad for me," Kaitlin teased.

"Well, it is for me," Kyle teased her back. "I think you may have eaten one too many sandwiches."

Kaitlin swatted him on the arm and said, "Give me that key before I change my mind."

Kaitlin placed the string with the key around her neck, and once again, Kyle hoisted her up so that she was at eye level with the holes. This time, he had thought ahead enough to realize that he needed to position both of them close enough to the wall that she could actually put the key in the holes. Kyle was unable to look up while he was holding her, but he sensed that she was getting a little wobbly. He realized she must be taking the key off from around her neck.

"Can you reach it?" he asked.

"Yep, I can," Kaitlin responded.

Kyle heard the sound of the key rubbing against the wall as she tried to slide it into its place in the holes. He felt more movement from her above him and he asked her, "What's going on up there?"

Kaitlin shouted, "IT FITS!"

She wobbled again because she had been so excited at her discovery that out of habit, she almost jumped for joy. Kyle had to steady her to keep her from falling, which turned out to be no easy task. Once he did, he called up to her, "Are you able to turn it?"

"I think so," Kaitlin answered, and Kyle felt her moving about again. He heard a strange sound, similar to the clicking sound he would hear when a key is turned in a door and the lock is released.

The wall close to where he stood gave way like a door and slowly moved out and away from the rest of the wall. It swung open so wide that had it not been for their quick reflexes, the two of them would have been crushed by the heavy stone. Kaitlin was forced to jump off of Kyle's shoulders and Kyle lunged out of the way. When the door stopped moving, it was open approximately two-thirds of the way to the wall behind it. Kyle and Kaitlin sat there on the ground, staring at the open doorway. Kyle stood up quickly and moved directly in front of the open area.

"I wonder how that door was able to swing open like that," Kaitlin mused.

"I'm not sure, but I'm going to find out," Kyle replied, and he made a move to examine the inner workings of the door. However, something caught Kyle's attention before he had time to make it to the door.

Kaitlin watched as Kyle's eyes traveled slowly up the length of an object behind the door and traveled to just below the ceiling.

"That's a sarcophagus!" Kyle shouted excitedly.

Kaitlin backed up and said, "If that's what it is, I don't think I want to go near it."

Kyle stepped close to the sarcophagus and ran his hand over it.

"How high do you think that is?" Kaitlin asked.

Kyle glanced up and down to figure out the approximate height of the thing. "Well," he finally answered, "it looks like it's about as tall as two of you and two of me together. So," he finished, "I would have to guess that it's approximately twenty feet tall."

"Wow!" Kaitlin said with her mouth gaping. Indeed, it was quite a sight to behold. Kaitlin inched forward ever so slightly and asked, "Whose tomb do you think that is, anyway?"

"I really have no idea," Kyle answered, "but I'm sure going to check it out. I wonder how this thing opens."

He stepped to the side of the sarcophagus and examined it. There were two latches that kept it closed. One was at a height that Kyle could reach himself, but the other was approximately the same height as the key hole had been.

"Kaitlin, my friend," Kyle said suggestively, "I could use a hand again." He grinned at her and said, "Please. Pretty please."

"Oh no, not again!" Kaitlin said, shaking her head.

"Oh, come on!" Kyle said. "We've gotten this far. Please don't let me walk away from here without seeing what is in this thing."

"Fine!" Kaitlin said and sighed. Kyle undid the first latch. It sprung open easily, as if it had only been closed for ten years rather than perhaps thousands. Then he hefted Kaitlin onto his shoulders and she repeated the process with the second latch. She jumped down just as the lid of the sarcophagus swung open.

The first thing Kyle noticed was what appeared to be a very large bone of some sort. He studied it momentarily and realized that it was a leg bone. It turned out that there were actually two of them, each one separate, but as he looked a little further up, he noticed that they were connected. At the bottom of each leg bone there was an enormous foot attached.

Right about the time that Kyle was putting two and two together, Kaitlin shouted, "Oh, my gosh, Kyle, we've found a gigantic skeleton!"

Kyle took a few steps back and viewed the skeleton as a whole. He had been correct in his estimation that it was about four times the height of either one of them. The skeleton absolutely towered over them. The head of the skeleton was large enough to compare to at least the size of four human heads, if not more. Kyle had never seen anything like it, not even in his archaeology books.

"Kyle," Kaitlin said, sounding breathless and in awe, "what are we going to do now?"

Kyle, who was still absolutely stunned from their discovery, replied, "We're going to do nothing! The only thing that we're going to do now is leave and never come back to this place!"

"*What*??" a startled Kaitlin asked. "Why? Don't we need to tell somebody that we found this?"

"No!" Kyle responded sharply. "This is someone's final resting place. It would be wrong on so many levels to disturb it any more than we already have!"

Kaitlin handed Kyle the key that had opened the door and which had allowed them to make this amazing discovery. "What about the professor, though?" she asked Kyle. "Shouldn't we at least tell *him* what we found?"

"Kaitlin," Kyle answered her slowly, "it just doesn't seem right to have people poking and prodding at this skeleton just to find some answers. This was a *person* at one time. Imagine how you would feel if this was one of your relatives and people wanted to use them for experiments."

Kaitlin looked up and noticed that one of the fingers was missing from the skeleton's right hand. "I understand, Kyle," she said slowly, "but it looks as if the professor already has a part of this skeleton." She pointed to where the finger was missing.

Kyle looked at the mouth and noticed that there was also a tooth missing. "Good for him," Kyle replied snippily. "He has enough. Now let's get out of here and go home and pretend like we never even found this thing."

CHAPTER 22

School was finally over. Kyle had spent the first few days of vacation wandering around the beach. He had tried to talk himself into going back into the cave but was never capable of following through. He sat on the beach, staring at the waves for hours at a time. Occasionally, he would glance over at the rock wall and think about the day he and Kaitlin had found the giant skeleton. He reasoned with himself that he had made the right decision. However, something the professor had said about people needing to know the truth would not leave him. The professor had said that if a discovery like this were to come to light, then it may cause people to have more faith in their Creator.

Kyle knew that the professor was right. He reasoned that if there was proof of a being that corroborated what the Bible said, then at least *some* people would have their eyes opened to the truth. However, he still struggled with disturbing the final resting place of the person who was entombed in the recess of the cave wall.

Kaitlin had been pacing around her house during those days, hoping with everything in her to be able to talk to her friend. On the third day of break, the suspense finally became too much for her and she had ridden her bike out to the beach. When she saw Kyle sitting there, staring out at the ocean, she had realized that he needed some time to process all of his thoughts and emotions. So she stood there in the parking lot, watching him and praying for him to have wisdom. Kyle never once noticed she was there, but she didn't mind. She knew that soon he would be able to talk about the cave and what they had found. And when he was ready, she would be there for him. In the meantime, she asked God to show her how to help her friend.

****

It was the first Friday after summer break had begun, and Kaitlin was feeling lazy. She had slept in until 11 a.m. and then had sat in her living room watching TV. Her parents were both at work, so she was left alone to entertain herself. The last few days had been very difficult for her. She missed her friend, and longed to be able to talk to him. As far as she could tell, Kyle had been able to see his dad a little more. For that she was very grateful. She sighed and thought that even though she was happy for Kyle and his dad, she still wished that Kyle would come talk to her. She realized that wishing wasn't going to change anything, so she determined that she was going to make the most out of her day.

She went to the kitchen to make lunch for herself and found a leftover casserole in the refrigerator. She dished some out on a plate and popped it into the microwave to reheat it. While she was waiting for the food to finish cooking, she went into the living room to see what programs were playing on TV. She flipped through the channels and found that there really wasn't much on that she was interested in watching. She left the TV playing and walked back into the kitchen to retrieve her casserole. Just as she was opening the door of the microwave, she heard the doorbell ring.

She hollered out, "Just a minute," and scurried to the mirror in the hallway. Her hair was a mess because she hadn't showered yet, so she quickly combed her fingers through it. The doorbell rang again. "I'll be right there!" she hollered, as she put the finishing touches on her hair. Finally, she threw her hands up in the air in utter defeat (*Hair 1, Kaitlin 0,* she thought), and then she ran to answer the door. When she pulled the door open, there stood Kyle with a slight grin on his face.

"Are you busy?" he asked.

"Never too busy for my best friend!" Kaitlin replied. "I was just about to have some lunch. Have you eaten yet?"

"No, actually, I haven't," Kyle responded. "I am pretty hungry. I never got around to eating breakfast."

"Well, if you don't mind casserole, I am more than willing to share."

Kyle made a funny face and asked, "What's in it?"

Kaitlin laughed at his expression and answered, "I know that Mom has made some pretty strange casseroles, but this one is normal. I promise. This one is only a spaghetti casserole."

"Oh, all right then," Kyle responded.

Kaitlin grabbed an extra plate out of the cupboard and heated up another helping of casserole.

"Hey," she said, "why don't we take this outside and sit at the picnic table. I've been cooped up in here all morning."

"Really?" Kyle asked in a teasing voice. "It looks to me like you just woke up!"

"I've been up for hours!" Kaitlin replied with feigned disgust. Kyle gave her a look that said he didn't believe her. "Fine," Kaitlin said, peeking at the clock in the kitchen, "I guess it's only been about an hour."

"That's my Kaitlin!" Kyle said with a huge grin. "You never have been one to get up at the crack of dawn. I always wonder if your mom has to literally drag you out of bed for school," he finished with a laugh.

"Oh, hush!" Kaitlin said, and swatted him.

They each grabbed their own plate and a fork and headed outside. The two of them sat down at the picnic table and began to eat their food in silence. Chester was out in the yard and had been doing his usual routine of sniffing, first the air, and then the grass. He caught the scent of a squirrel and gave chase. He ran behind Kyle so abruptly, and barking so loudly, that a startled Kyle nearly poked himself in the mouth with his fork. Kaitlin laughed so hysterically at the scene before her that she nearly inhaled the bite of the pasta she had just taken.

Once Kyle was over being so startled, he asked Kaitlin, "Am I going to have to do the Heimlich maneuver on you?"

Kaitlin coughed and sputtered and really couldn't speak, but she shook her head no.

"Well, that's a relief," Kyle said, teasing her.

Kaitlin swallowed hard and said, "No, really, I'm fine." Then after a pause, she looked at her little dog, who had ambled over to the table, and said, "Thanks a lot, Chester!"

"Oh, don't be too hard on him," Kyle admonished her. "He did keep Anthony from stealing the key and the tooth after all. Which reminds me..." And here Kyle held up a finger as if to say, "I'll be right back." He went through the gate into his own front yard and was gone for a couple of minutes. When he returned, he was carrying the treasure chest with him.

He set it down on the table and opened the lid. The key was lying in the very top of the treasure chest and Kaitlin noticed that Kyle was no longer trying to cover the key with tissues to hide it. He pulled the key out of the chest and held it up for Kaitlin to see.

"I've been doing a lot of thinking for the last few days," he began.

Kaitlin interrupted him to say, "Yeah, I've noticed . . ."

Kyle gave her a look, wondering what she meant, but then continued on. "I've decided that . . ."

Again, Kaitlin interrupted him. "Kyle, do you really mean to keep this discovery all to yourself? I don't think it would be fair if—"

This time it was Kyle's turn to interrupt her. He said, "Kaitlin, I was going to tell you that I've decided that the professor is right." Kaitlin said nothing, and her jaws hung wide open in disbelief. Now that Kyle truly had her attention, he continued, "This is much too important of a discovery to keep locked up (pun intended). After this weekend is over, I am going to send a text message to the professor. I will tell him about what we found, and I will ask him to meet with me. When we meet, I plan to give him this," Kyle said, indicating the key.

Kaitlin jumped up out of her seat, threw her arms around Kyle, and said, "I knew you would do the right thing!"

****

As it turned out, Kyle did not have to wait until the weekend was over to find the professor. After having lunch with Kaitlin, Kyle had returned home to see his dad for a bit before he left for work. His dad was in the kitchen preparing a dinner to take to work with him. Kyle had gone upstairs to put the treasure chest in his closet, where he was storing it until he could give the key to the professor. Suddenly, the doorbell chimed. Kyle made his way to the top of the stairs to go open the door, but his dad beat him there. Kyle heard the door open and then heard his dad ask, "How can I help you, sir?"

Kyle heard the familiar German accent of the professor, who answered, "Sir, I apologize, but I must speak with young Kyle."

Kyle's dad was taken aback and took a moment to answer. Kyle took this opportunity to rescue the situation as much as he possibly could. During the last few days he had meant to tell his dad the whole story about the cave. He had enjoyed their time together so much that he just hadn't gotten around to it. He had thought that he may be able to explain everything over the weekend—*before* he went to see the professor and give him the key. But now it was too late, and Kyle could only hope that his dad wouldn't be too upset with him when he heard the story of the cave. He ran down the stairs, skipping every other step, and got to the front door before his dad could utter a word.

"Hello, Professor Von Lichtenspiel," he said in greeting.

"Ah, young Kyle, I am so glad to see you. I must speak with you at once," the professor answered.

"I was going to come find you on Monday," Kyle answered him.

Kyle's dad watched the exchange between the older man and his son. When he was finally able to speak, he asked, "Kyle, what's this all about?"

Instead of allowing Kyle to speak on his own behalf, the professor jumped in and said, "Sir, you have a very fine young man for a son. Please sit down and I will explain everything."

Mr. Marshall did not look convinced, but he sat down on the living room couch and motioned for the professor to sit as well.

"You see . . ." the professor began, and he related the story that his friend, the archaeologist, had told him so long ago. He explained that he had come to their town specifically to explore the cave and see if the legend that had been passed down for generations was true after all. He proceeded to explain that he began seeing Kyle go into the cave starting a few months ago

"My nephew, Anthony, and I kept a close watch on young Kyle, sir. We knew that he was determined to explore that cave, and we thought that he might be likely to find out the secret of the cave long before we would. Young Kyle here is very brave indeed, Meester Marshall."

Right in the middle of the professor's account of the story, the doorbell rang again. This time when Kyle answered the door, Kaitlin was standing there.

"I saw the professor at the door and I figured you might need some moral support," she said.

"Thank you, Kaitlin!" Kyle said, with a sigh of relief. "You just may be a life saver!" he said, peeking over at his dad.

Kaitlin smiled a wary smile and then stepped into the living room. "Hello, Mr. Marshall," she said in greeting. Kyle thought she sounded much braver than he felt right then. After all, she was just as at risk of getting into a world of trouble as he was.

"Hello, Kaitlin," Kyle's dad responded, and then he nodded toward the professor and said, "Please continue, Professor."

The professor explained in great detail how Kyle had first found the tooth. He went on to tell Mr. Marshall about the Star Room and how they had all met for the first time. He continued on with details about the discoveries that Kyle and Kaitlin had made, even the ones that had occurred since the time that Kyle had given the professor the tooth to study.

Kyle interjected, "Dad, in one room, we found a finger bone that was at least three times the size of your finger. I always thought *you* had big hands, but this was enormous! And then Anthony stole the finger right out of my hand!"

The professor gave Kyle a sad look. "*Ja*, young Kyle, I am indeed very sorry for the actions of my nephew! He should have never done such a thing!"

Kyle nodded his head and assured the professor, "It's all right. I'm glad you have it, so you can study it."

"Study it?" Kyle's dad asked, surprised.

"*Ja*, Meester Marshall. We believe that this finger bone and the tooth that your son found are from a very large being. We believe that these two are proof that there really were giants, known as Nephilim, that comingled and lived among the humans as the Bible has talked about. I am doing many studies to prove that this theory is correct."

At this point, Kyle jumped in. "Uh, Professor, I have something more to tell you about. I found something else that you can run some tests on . . ."

"*Ja*, young Kyle," the professor interrupted, "I know that you found a key. I am sure that once we find out where the key fits, we will find our greatest discovery yet."

The professor barely got the words out of his mouth before Kyle blurted out, "Kaitlin and I already found it!"

"Found what?" his dad and the professor asked in unison.

Kyle looked at Kaitlin and said, "You tell them."

Kaitlin looked uncertain, but she finally spoke these words very softly and slowly, "We found a giant skeleton."

After this revelation, the professor, who was obviously stunned, asked how they had finally found the skeleton. Kyle and Kaitlin took turns relating their journey through the pool and the tunnel, as well as the exploration of the room with the very high ceiling.

"I just knew there was something special about that room!" Kyle said, excitedly.

Kaitlin chimed in, saying, "I'm glad he did, because I was about ready to throw in the towel."

The professor looked confused, but then he asked, "Were you going to throw your towel in the pool?"

Kyle and Kaitlin laughed hysterically, and then Kyle explained, "No, Professor, that expression means that she was just about to give up searching the room."

The professor smiled and said, "Well, then, young Kyle, I certainly am glad that you weren't willing to throw the towel in!"

"Me too!" Kyle agreed, and smiled at the professor's mix-up of the phrase.

Kyle's dad decided that he would have to be a little bit late getting to work that evening. He invited the professor to meet his wife when she returned home from work and asked him to stay for dinner. He even invited Kaitlin to stay for dinner.

"Oh, boy, Dad, you don't know what you've gotten us into!" Kyle said with a wink at Kaitlin. "This girl might eat us out of house and home!"

Kaitlin gave him a look as if she were shooting daggers at him, and Kyle closed his mouth.

At dinner, Kyle looked around the table at the faces gathered there. He was thankful that this was the way it had worked out. Neither his dad nor his mom seemed like they were mad at him for exploring in the cave on his own.

At one point, his dad had even pulled him aside and said, "Son, I'm sorry that I was never able to explore that cave with you. I am *very* proud of my brave son, though!"

Kyle's eyes had watered for just a moment after his dad had said that. All he could manage to choke out was, "Thanks, Dad."

They all decided that the professor would gather a team together, and they would begin excavation of the giant from the cave first thing on Monday morning. Kyle handed the key over to the professor, saying, "Here, you might need this."

The professor took the key from Kyle's hand and patted him on the back. "Well, done, young Kyle. You have made all of us very proud. Not only that, but you will now go down in history as someone who found one of the greatest discoveries of all time."

CHAPTER 23

One week later, the professor contacted Kyle by sending him a text message. "Young Kyle," he wrote, "I would like to speak with you about something. Will you meet me at the cave?"

Kyle texted him back: "*Ja*, Professor, I will meet you there. I will bring Kaitlin with me."

"That is fine," the professor replied. "I shall arrive tomorrow at 9:00 a.m."

"OK, Professor, see you then," Kyle responded. Kyle had to wonder why the professor wanted to meet him at the cave. Excavation of the skeleton from the cave had been underway for several days now.

Kyle had thought that by now they should actually be fairly close to being able to remove him (or her). Kyle realized that he didn't have enough knowledge to help him determine whether the bones were from a male or female. Apparently, that was something the professor would be able to accomplish when he ran his tests. Kyle was somewhat anxious to find out the results of the tests. He had a difficult time imagining that giant as a woman, but he supposed it would be highly unlikely that all Nephilim were male.

Kyle sent a text message to Kaitlin: "Kaitlin, do you have a few minutes to come over?"

It was not long before he received a reply that said, "Absolutely! I'll be right over."

Kyle sat in his living room, waiting for the front doorbell to ring. He fiddled with his phone, looking again at the text message from the professor. He was puzzled, and to be honest, it was driving him absolutely crazy wondering what the professor wanted to talk about. He had slipped into deep thought, pondering many theories as to the possible reasons that the professor might want to meet him at the cave. The doorbell rang and startled him. He jumped up off of the couch and ran to the front door. There stood Kaitlin, grinning from ear to ear.

"Hey, Kyle," she said in greeting. "Thanks for asking me to come over. I've been wondering if you had heard from our German friend."

"I did," Kyle answered. "He really didn't *tell* me anything except that he wanted to meet at the cave tomorrow morning. I was hoping you might want to come with me."

"I'D LOVE TO!" Kaitlin nearly shrieked. "Are you kidding me? Of course I'll be there!"

Kyle smiled, giving her a look that told her he was about to tell her something she wouldn't be very happy with.

"*What?*" Kaitlin asked. "I've seen that look before, and it usually means trouble!"

Kyle laughed. "I wouldn't say it's trouble," he began, "but I'm afraid that you're not going to be very happy about it."

"Oh, gee whiz, Kyle," Kaitlin said in an extremely frustrated voice, "just tell me!"

"Fine," Kyle began. "Two words: nine a.m."

Kaitlin looked taken aback. "You mean that I have to be out of bed by nine o'clock, right?" she asked imploringly.

"No, Kaitlin," Kyle answered with the biggest, cheesiest grin she had ever seen him wear, "we have to *be there* by nine."

Kaitlin looked deflated. To Kyle, it looked as if she were wondering if she had spoken too soon by agreeing to meet him and the professor at the cave. She finally spoke, and with sincere conviction, she said, "You were right. I don't like it at all! That's like having to get up for school!" Here she sighed, and then continued, "But this is very important, so I promise that I will be there on time."

"Great!" Kyle said excitedly. "I can't imagine being there without you. After all, you were just as much a part of the discoveries as I was."

****

The next morning, Kyle and Kaitlin rode to the cave together. Kyle had been surprised to see Kaitlin waiting in his driveway, already seated on her bike and ready to go. Kyle had longed to tease her, but he just couldn't bring himself to do it. He was actually very proud of her for sticking to her word, especially knowing how difficult it had been for her. Kaitlin had asked him if he had figured out what the professor wanted. Kyle just shrugged and said, "No idea."

They arrived at the beach and noticed that there were quite a few cars in the parking lot. It seemed a bit surprising, but Kyle reasoned that school was out and there were probably many parents who brought their kids to the beach on such a beautiful day.

Kyle looked at Kaitlin and said, "I just realized that the professor never told me specifically *where* he wanted to meet. I guess maybe we should just go in through the back entrance. I have a feeling that once we are inside, we will find him." Kaitlin nodded in agreement.

The two friends set off and made their way up the back path and into the cave. They went to the tunnels that led to the Pillar Room first, but when they arrived, there was no sign of the professor. Kaitlin called out, "Professor, we're here. Where are you?"

Kyle thought he heard the professor's voice off in the distance, but it was so faint that it was hard to tell. "Did you hear that?" he asked Kaitlin.

"Hear what?" she asked.

"I thought I heard him," Kyle responded. "If we're quiet, I bet we'll hear him." They both listened intently and finally Kyle perked up. "There," he said, pointing. "It sounds like he may be in the Star Room."

They wound through various tunnels and rooms until they made it to the Star Room. As it turned out, Kyle had been right. The professor was in this room. Kyle looked around and realized that it was in this very room that they had first met the professor. So much had transpired between then and now that it almost seemed like that day had happened many years ago.

The professor walked over to where Kyle and Kaitlin stood. He shook Kyle's hand and gave Kaitlin a hug. "I am so glad to see the two of you!" the professor exclaimed. "I have some very exciting news for you!"

Kyle and Kaitlin exchanged puzzled looks. Kaitlin was the first one to speak, and she asked the professor, "What is it?"

The professor rubbed his hands together like a child who was about to receive a present for Christmas. "Well, my two brave young ones, we have received a request from a museum that is near my hometown. They would like to display the skeleton there for everyone to see. They would also like to display the finger bone and the tooth and key that you found, young Kyle. They plan to write a short story which describes how you found these incredible artifacts. The story will be displayed in a case along with those three objects."

"Wow! That is pretty cool!" Kaitlin said in an excited voice.

Kyle, however, did not have much to say. He had figured that this outcome was likely, but there was a part of him that was disappointed that the skeleton would reside in a museum that was so far away. Kyle sighed, and the professor heard him.

"Ah, I understand that exhale all too well," the professor told Kyle.

Kaitlin interjected, "He means 'sigh,' Kyle."

Kyle was about to say, "I already know what he means," but he figured it didn't really matter. Instead, he turned to the professor and said, "I hope that someday I will get to visit the museum."

"Oh, *ja*," the professor answered quickly, "I nearly forgot to tell you! The museum has agreed to pay for you and your family and Miss Kaitlin and her family to fly to Germany and see the unveiling of the skeleton."

Kyle was astounded at the professor's revelation. "Is this for real?" he asked him.

"Absolutely!" the professor answered. "The unveiling will occur in one month's time, and you, Miss Kaitlin, and your families will all be there for it!"

"That's fantastic!" Kaitlin shouted. "Kyle, we're going to get to travel across the world!"

"That is pretty amazing," Kyle agreed.

The professor rubbed his hands together once more, and as he did, he announced, "This is not the only news I have for you!"

Kyle could not possibly imagine what other surprises the professor could have up his sleeve, but he said, "OK, Professor, I'll bite. What else would you like to tell us?"

The professor looked gravely concerned and did not speak for several moments. When he did, he replied, "Young Kyle, you are not a dog! Why would you bite me? Have I made you angry?"

Kyle and Kaitlin both burst out laughing so hard that they were doubled over. This made the professor worry even more. He looked somewhat agitated, as if he were ready to flee the room.

"Oh, Professor, no . . ." Kyle assured him. "That is only an expression! It just means that I am willing to listen to what you have to say." In spite of himself, Kyle just could not help smiling at the fact that the professor had taken him so literally.

"Oh, *ja*, now I see," the professor said, but he still looked a bit confused and unsure.

Kyle decided it was time to bring the topic back around to the other news the professor wanted to share with them. "So, Professor," he began, "you were saying . . ."

The professor nodded his head and said, "The other news is this: Word has spread about the giant skeleton that you have found. A woman contacted me yesterday morning and said that she was with a local TV station. They asked if they could do an interview with the two of you."

Kyle looked absolutely bewildered and was temporarily unable to speak. A thought occurred to him that this might explain all the cars they had seen in the parking lot earlier. Kyle, who was not one to have attention drawn to him, said, "Uh-uh! No way! I am not going to be doing any television interviews. Not today, and not any day! Besides, I think my parents would be unhappy about this."

"Kyle, are you *crazy*?" Kaitlin asked. "This is the chance of a lifetime!"

"It is indeed, my young friend!" the professor agreed. "Kyle, if you are brave enough to explore this cave, you are certainly brave enough to speak to a few reporters."

Kyle heard the word "few" and looked like he was ready to run out with his tail between his legs.

"He's right," Kaitlin said, "and you know it. Kyle, you can do this. If you want, I will stand right beside you."

Kyle looked at Kaitlin gratefully, and then he turned to address the professor. "All right," he responded, "but I still don't think my parents will like this one bit!"

"Ah," the professor answered, "you have nothing to worry about. I spoke with them yesterday and they gave their approval."

With that argument quashed, Kyle could only say, "OK, then let's do this." They followed the professor through the cave until they came upon the front entrance.

"You'll be fine, Kyle," Kaitlin reassured him. "I'll be right by your side the whole time."

Kyle took her hand and they stepped out to the clicking of cameras.

****

The press conference had finally ended, and Kyle had to admit that it hadn't been that bad after all. He remembered that at one point he had looked out among the gathered crowd and he had spotted his parents waving to him. Kyle had instantly felt relieved and his confidence had grown exponentially when he saw their smiling faces. He had bravely faced the questions of the reporters. One by one, he had answered them, and he had even somehow had the ability to launch into the story of how he and Kaitlin had made their discoveries.

After the reporters began to pack up their belongings to leave, Kyle's parents had approached him. His dad had given him a strong handshake and said, "Kyle, we are incredibly proud of you!"

His mom, on the other hand, had tears streaming down her face as she gave him her Mama Bear hug.

"What's wrong, Mom?" Kyle asked.

"Oh, nothing is wrong," she responded. "I'm just amazed by the young man that you are turning out to be!"

Kaitlin had chuckled, and whispered to Kyle, "You know how emotional moms can be."

"Who are you kidding?" Kyle asked in disbelief. "All of you 'women' are emotional!"

"So true!" Kaitlin agreed.

The professor walked over to the group. "Kyle, may I speak with you and Kaitlin alone?"

Kyle's mom nodded her head in approval, and Kyle and Kaitlin followed the professor as he stepped in front of the mouth of the cave.

"I understand," he said, "that you must feel somewhat sad now that you have finished your exploration of this cave."

"Yes," Kyle agreed. "I have felt a little empty knowing that it's all over."

"Well, my young friend," the professor said with a smile, "what if I told you that this really wasn't the end, but only a new beginning?"

"What are you saying, Professor?" Kaitlin asked.

The professor pointed to the rock wall in the opposite direction of where they now stood. Kyle looked at the professor, understanding what he was trying to tell him. Kyle's face lit up like it never had before.

"Professor, do you mean to say that there's another . . ." Kaitlin asked.

But before she could finish, Kyle took off running in the direction that the professor had pointed. Kaitlin looked at the professor, and then at Kyle, and said, "Hey, Kyle, wait for me!"

About the Author

KRISTIN TUCKER is a 45-year-old Rockford, Illinois native who became enamored with reading at a young age. She began writing poetry at the age of twelve and has continued to write poems ever since. In her mid-twenties, she realized that in addition to her passion for poetry, she had a strong desire to craft a novel.

Prior to having her own children, Kristin attended Southwest Baptist University with the intent of getting a degree in Youth Ministry. During a summer break, Kristin interned with a local church and was amazed by the faith displayed in the young teens. Although she never made a career of youth ministry, that experience fueled her desire to see children of all ages surrounded with people and experiences that would strengthen their faith.

Kristin realized the important role that books played in her life as a Pre-teen and Teenager and how they played a large part in shaping the person she is. With this in mind, she wrote *The Secret in the Cliffs*, in which she blends adventure, humor, and the story of an adolescent boy that endeavors to live his life according to his faith.

Kristin is married to her loving husband, Greg. They each have their own businesses but feel blessed to be able to work together daily. Between the two of them, they have three children: Megan, Joshua, and Jacob.

You can find Kristin on Facebook, Twitter, and LinkedIn.